1

The Whole Stunned World

World

Between Boston and Burma

By Jenny Ruth Yasi

Hpo Nyo realized that this was a bird rarely seen anywhere near a town; it had been blown in by the storm. If it did revive, he could not just release the bird from the roof, as it would be lost and bewildered among the unfamiliar houses and buildings. He would have to make a special trip into the countryside to set it free (from "The Day the Weather Broke," U Win Pe, <u>Inked Over Ripped Out: Burmese Storytellers and the Censors</u>, p. 42).

Notes and dedication: All the major political events depicted in this story are based on true events. The quotes of Luther and Johnny, who are actual people, are actual quotations taken from published interviews. Gurney's Pitta is a real rare bird.

Dedicated to the people of Burma. And for editorial assistance and her incredible relationship with Burma, to Edith Mirante; also for inspiration, to Simon Billenness; to the Irrawaddy Magazine, Free Burma!, all the artists, healers, craftspeople, NGO's and non-profits whose tireless efforts not only save many lives, but also protect the environment, freedom of thought, and freedom of expression. To all who struggle for peace in a violent world, to all those forced to endure injustice; to Min Ko Naing, to Aung San Suu Kyi, peace be always with you.

For more information, see
www.freeburmacoalition.org
www.freeburmarangers.org
www.burmacampaign.org.uk
www.uscampaignforburma.org

Chapter One: Cambridge Massachusetts
August 1999

Bobby opened the carved wooden dresser, pushed his hand under his mother's mysterious undergarments. She had pink and black bras, lace stockings, and silk panties, perfumes and powder. It was as if she was in the room.

It was late August; school would start up again soon. Bobby's mother, Gurney (named after a rare Asian bird), was out jogging on Boston Commons. Robert the father wasn't home yet from work.

Nothing special was under the bed or in the closet; he'd checked there last week. On the bedside table there was a book about the Buddha, and in the bedside drawer were tubes of ointment, massage oil, and a yellow plastic case with a weird rubber disc inside.

Bobby had no idea what he expected to find, but some sort of weapon might be cool. Like, maybe a grenade. Rickie would flip. Or, he thought, she might have a photograph of a man, carrying a grenade. Bobby suffered a hopeful dread that his mother might have something like that.

He searched, but found nothing. Nothing in her sock drawer either. Bobby put everything more-or-less back into place.

Gurney wasn't very good at keeping secrets, but the obvious way she tried to delay his introduction to the scary things of the world made Bobby anxious. Sometimes he thought he was born with a built-in secret-detector, and he'd automatically know and stumble onto whatever questions she didn't want him to ask.

"Why is the file cabinet locked?"

"I'm not hiding anything Bobby, they're just old photographs from Burma. I'll go over the whole stack when you're older."

"Maybe it's worse in my imagination. I want to see them."

"Well look at these ones, right here on the wall."

"What about Maung?" He asked her this directly. "Why don't you have any pictures of him?"

She always had the same answer, that the only photographs she could save were taken after Maung went missing.

Bobby knew about the people she'd loved in Burma as though they still were alive, as though they all shared the family townhouse in Boston. He knew that Maung was funny, smart, and taught his mother how to make coconut curry. Bobby squirmed, pulled loose fibers in the bedspread fabric. "Like, that poem Maung wrote. I love that poem about Grandpa."

"Me too." Gurney read the poem to him till he had it memorized.

"Was he sorta like me?"

Gurney squinted, looked at him a long time, pulled his ears out, clipped her fingers over his forehead. She laughed and admitted, "Your grandfather looked sort of like a wino, like Grizzly Adams, with less beard, and less teeth. But you've certainly inherited his attitude."

Bobby rephrased his question carefully. "What I really meant was Maung. I bet I look more like Maung than I look like Daddy. "

Gurney closed her eyes and said, "I can't even remember what Maung looked like."

Bobby tugged a drawer, getting it open with a bang, rattling the handle of a jewelry box that was set on top of the dresser. He'd never paid much attention to this jewelry box before. Mahogany with a brass clasp and shaped like a flower, it was locked. The dresser-mirror shook, the whole bureau shook (it was old and fragile), as he fiddled with the lid.

Smooth-skinned, glossy-haired, Bobby's black eyes folded deeply, more so than his mother's, whose eyes were an unusual green; leaf-like eyes. Gurney's skin was also almond-colored, lighter than Bobby's. People told him that he took after his mother, but it worried him to look in the mirror, and find nothing in his own face, in his own skin, that also resembled his father. Almost every day, someone asked what country he came from. He'd answer Boston, and they'd laugh. All through third and fourth grades, his next-door-neighbor and sometime best friend Rickie believed Bobby's story, that he was actually an alien from another planet! When he was in the right mood, he liked the way he looked. He liked that he was different.

But now Bobby wasn't a little kid anymore, he was 11 years old and in the sixth grade, old enough to think about things like genetics and to wonder how an Asian-American mother, and a Scottish-English father, could wind up with a throw back as Burmese looking as this?

"What are you doing?"

Bobby jumped as his mother pushed open the bedroom door. She walked over to where he was standing with one hand still on her jewelry box.

Why did he always wind up doing the wrong thing and getting caught? It didn't make any sense. Other kids never get caught.

Gurney sat down on the edge of the bed.

Bobby leaned his head onto her shoulder. "I'm sorry," he whispered.

Her back stiff, she glanced at him from the corner of her eye, damp hair clinging to her face, still flushed and sweaty from running. "What are you looking for? Again? " But he didn't have words to describe why he was doing this, or this increasing sense of being displaced, of belonging somewhere else and to something else, that he felt hanging over his life. Another thing he did that he wasn't supposed to do was ask test questions, testing to see if she was telling him the truth. He had gotten into trouble for it before, but he'd also gotten better at it.

"What part of me takes after Daddy?"

"Your attitude," she said, and laughed, ruffled his hair, smiled and sighed. "No, you're right. You don't look much like Daddy, for sure. Is this that stage where you're wondering if you're adopted?" His mother's tone of voice had a faintly detectable overtone of laughing at a joke that's not funny. "But nooooooo," she tickled him. "Of course not! But you certainly take after your grandmother's side of the family!"

7

Emotion washed over him. The feeling that was forming, hardening in his throat, was scaring and embarrassing him. "Everyone thinks I'm stupid!"

"Maybe you should cut your hair," his mother said. "Maybe kids make fun because they can't tell if you're a boy or a girl."

Bobby elbowed her. She was leaning on him.

"Oh, come on. I'm only teasing. You know what you are. It doesn't matter what anyone else thinks," she said, and bounced a bit on the edge of the bed, trying to get him to smile. "Right?"

Bobby nodded, wiped his nose on his sleeve.

"Male," he said, and sniffed. He sighed. "I'm a Burmese male, 11 years old, 5 foot 1."

"Burmese-American," Gurney corrected. "And Burmese people are so very beautiful. Handsome." She kissed his cheek. Gurney petted the skin under his chin. "When you're a bit older, girls will go wild over you. " She thought for a moment, then added "You'll be tall like your father."

Bobby looked into the mirror, watched his mother's oval face lengthen as she shook her head. "You look in the mirror too much. You're vain." She tried to tickle him into looking away.

"Mumma, please." He said, "Just tell me the truth."

The instant he said it, he knew he had something right, and that all this time she'd been lying to him. The corners of her eyes lifted, but she didn't dare look at him. He squeezed her arm, harder and harder, till he dented her flesh with his fingernails and tears rose along the lower rims of her shapely eyes, down bridge of her nose, onto her lips, and she flinched away.

Urban noises penetrated the walls. A plane was passing overhead. The dishwasher was running in the kitchen.

"My birthday was May 27, 1989. Is that part right?" He'd never felt so angry.

She nodded. "7:58 in the morning."

"What happened to your parents, and Maung, and how you left Burma -- that part is true?"

"Why would anyone lie about a thing like that? Don't make this a crime scene Bobby," she said. "We love you so much."

Over at least the past few years, Bobby had been figuring all this out, and what he needed to say, what he needed to ask. Most of what she would tell him he had already guessed in unconscious, remote parts of his mind. But it would change everything now when he knew. How could he be the same person anymore? He felt himself becoming someone else.

"I got out of Burma in September, and I met Daddy on the plane in October," she said, in a low chuckling, sniffling away the tears. "Everything happened so fast. I was under a lot of pressure."

"You said I was premature! You lied to me!"

"How do we know anything, Bobby?" Gurney leaned away, laughed lightly, rubbed her hands over her face, turned to him with a sober smile. "All mothers lie a little bit. It was something that didn't seem to matter."

Bobby exploded with rage, slapped his thighs and shouted, "It fucking matters Mom!"

"Bobby! Language!"

"You left Maung! You abandoned him!"

"I didn't!" she protested but he interrupted her.

"You did! I know you did!"

Gurney pushed him off her lap and stood to take deep breaths. "Oh my word Bobby," she sighed. "You're so young. You're supposed to be a child. Can't we just relax and have fun and enjoy our lucky lives?"

But then, leaning over the dresser, she slipped a key out from the edge of the mirror frame, fumbled and worked it into the jewelry box lock.

"Here," she said, and dumped the contents (a bundle of sealed envelopes, stuffed and addressed, covered with canceled stamps) into his lap.

"I tried to find him," she said, wiping her eyes as she spoke. "Daddy even helped me. We called, sent letters, did everything we could think of. See?" She sorted through his stack. "These are the responses I got from the Red Cross, the American Embassy in Thailand, Insein Prison. These are ones sent from refugee camps. Bobby I lost my whole family there. I lost so many people that I love. Maung is dead. They're all dead."

She told him this part of the story before.

"When the military junta claimed all the bodies, it was impossible. We all were paralyzed by it. Especially people in the pro-democracy movement, the junta took their bodies, because bodies are evidence, and they wanted all evidence to disappear. The dictatorship doesn't want to make any pro-democracy martyrs. The only thing I could do was leave."

"So. I guessed it right. Maung is my real father. Right?"

"Robert is your real father. Robert loves us. He has tried so hard to help us."

Bobby panted. The room was getting darker. She patted him on the back.

"Daddy knows?" The ticking clock matched his heartbeat.

"Yes," she said, sighed a noisy rush of breath. "Yes honey. Of course he does. "

Bobby could hardly believe what he was hearing. "Maung Naing is my real Daddy," he whispered to himself.

"Your real Daddy is Robert White, and he should be home any minute. I don't want to get angry now, but I'm not kidding. What matters most, Bobby? Teeny bits of DNA, or someone who would go to the end of the earth for you? Daddy loves you." Again Gurney's voice choked. "You can't imagine how much he loves you."

Bobby sobbed. "I'm sorry. Don't cry. I didn't mean to find out."

Gurney mopped their tears with the back of her hand. "Well, it's hard to believe, isn't it? Anyway, even I couldn't believe it! I was so young. It was quite lucky, to meet Daddy when I did. Honestly. It all happened so fast. "

"It must have been weird for Daddy."

"He loved me. He loved you. Nothing else mattered."

"A lot else matters," he said, but he wanted to believe her.

"Okay," she said. "It all matters." She looked into his eyes. He looked so much like Maung. He did. She swallowed, and planted several kisses on his forehead, smiled. "You've got a point."

Bobby plunged ahead with the scariest thing he could imagine. "Maybe we should do that paternity test thing," Bobby knew kids who had that kind of proof, "to be sure."

"Are you kidding? " Gurney laughed.

"Maybe," he said, full of terror and frustration, "maybe I should ask Daddy about this."

Gurney braced herself with her hands on her hips. "You'll still have to figure it out for yourself," she said.

"Did I hear someone mention Daddy?" And Robert came into the bedroom, pulling off his jacket, setting down his briefcase and smoothing the little hair he had left across the top of his head. Bobby jumped up, and the pile of airmail fell onto the floor.

"Oh," Robert said, "I'm sorry," and awkwardly he stooped, picking up envelopes, squinting, stuttering, "one of those, those, you know..." His legs seemed to give out as he crouched lower on the floor.

Gurney bent to help him, "Robert. Here. It's okay. Let me get those."

Bobby could see his father's face turning red. Robert turned from the mail, and focused blue eyes on Bobby. "I didn't know we were talking about this tonight. Are you okay?"

"Yeah, Dad," Bobby said.

Robert's ankles didn't seem capable of helping him to stand back up. "So, then. Any questions?" And he searched his son's tear-streaked face. Gurney put her hand on his shoulder. The clock began to gong. Six pm. Bobby took in his father's puzzled face saying, "I mean, of course I knew it mattered.... maybe more to you than to me..."

Bobby handed him the elastic band.

They bunched the letters, leaning shoulder to shoulder.

Bobby said, "There's a chance he's still alive?"

Robert said, "If there's ever anything we can do for him, we'll do it."

Chapter Two Rangoon, Burma. August 1988

That night, several armed officers including Officer Ywa (who they'd recently had to dinner), went through the neighborhood, banging on doors. Soldiers took Maung, and three others.

At first the Williams family wasn't too worried, it looked like political theatre, they thought, Maung is influential. People love poets. They'll let him go.

Then it dawned slowly that they might be wrong.

Maung was Gurney's sweet-tempered, doe-eyed, 24 year old assistant professor of poetry, co-chairperson of the Burmese Democratic Student Organization, Gurney's boyfriend, like a member of the family. Respectful, charming, idealistic in the most attractive sense of the word, physically very handsome, smart, and not merely intellectually, but emotionally. Maung thrilled Gurney's father especially. He actually told her that he hoped she'd marry him.

Last Sunday, Maung brought them flowers.

"From our garden," he said. "To thank you for your courage."

"What courage?"

"It must take a lot of courage for your family to be here."

As Maung became increasingly well known and well loved for his pro-democracy position, it was a socially risky friendship in a strained political environment. But they were an American family, used to enjoying freedom of association, it seemed the dictatorship was weakening. And Maung impressed them not only with the strength of the pro-democracy movement, but also with his own integrity. No one in the Willams family felt particularly worried about anything. They were used to the weird energy that was Burma.

And Gurney and Maung seemed born for each other. Gurney's mixed-blood beauty and sharp American worldliness were doubly potent beside Maung. The two brought out the best in each other. Maung's outspokenness, and Gurney's focus together would surely move mountains.

Mya answered him. "Life itself is risky."

"But you raised your child to be free thinking," Maung said. "It takes courage to cultivate an open mind."

Wallace shook his head. "All American babies are free thinking."

"That's not true and you know it Daddy."

Wallace laughed. "I was just checking to see if you were listening. Gurney, do you hear how much this young man loves you?"

"Don't treat us like patriots," Mya said. "It was Wallace's idea to bring me back here, and strictly financial reasoning. I wouldn't be here if it wasn't for him. "

It was true. Wallace had invested and lost a lot in Burma. He had practical personal reasons for being involved. And if love could be considered a practical reason, maybe Gurney did too.

Maung handed Mya the bouquet. It was awkwardly moving. "I just wanted to thank you so much for everything."

He'd been missing now for 12 hours.

The landlord, Saw Bo Ottama, came up the steps, banged on their door.

"Colonel Salai Tun has been arrested," the landlord informed them. He sounded exhausted, and showed them the front page of the state-run newspaper. It had a picture of the Colonel in shackles, and with a one-word caption, Traitor.

"All last year I went out of my way to get to know the Colonel," Wallace told Mya. "Well this is nerve-wracking."

"People are saying that they've taken quite a large number of people last night," the landlord said.

Wallace's hands started to shake.

"But General Than is our friend too," Mya tried to comfort him. "I don't think we have anything to worry about."

17

"General Than's never been that good a friend," Wallace said. Gurney was leaning her lanky body against the stove, stirring boiling noodles.

"Maung said this could happen," Gurney said. She sounded thoughtful, not worried. "He said the military might detain people to keep them from speaking at the rallies. And they'll let everyone go after the rallies are over."

"Okay," Mya said, and she helped Gurney get out the bowls, "Let's hope he's right."

After lunch, Wallace decided to call General Than, and ask about a missing mathematics professor, Wang Lee, who was diabetic, and would need his medicine if they had him.

"You didn't tell the General that Wang Lee is your friend, did you?" Mya asked.

Wallace got off the phone. "No," he said, "Just that I was asking on behalf of the University."

"Ok. Good."

"I didn't ask about anyone else."

"I'm glad. We can't risk that."

"Right, don't worry. But I said if they had a list of names, I'd post it for the families." Wallace kneaded the side of his neck. While his hair had become very gray over the past few years, his moustache was stained yellow with cigarettes.

"That sounds safe enough," Mya responded. "And General Than's tone of voice was friendly."

"Like always," Wallace said. "Not super friendly, but not unfriendly either. Formal. He said they didn't have anyone else. Just Salai Tun."

"Maybe what people have said to Saw Bo Ottama was wrong."

Gurney dressed in jeans, a cotton t-shirt, and sandals, and she was flushed and curled on the carved wooden day bed, chewing on her nails, melting in the heat. Wallace felt a lump in his throat. They should have gone back to Boston a month ago.

"You look sick," Mya said, sounding worried, and Wallace thought she was speaking to him.

"No, I'm fine," Gurney answered, and ripped off another bit of nail. "Just, I don't know what to do next. It's hard to do nothing. But I think Maung wants us to do nothing for a while."

"Maung's tougher than he looks," Wallace told her. "I wouldn't worry too much."

"I'm not worried about him. I'm worried about us."

Wallace moved beside his daughter, began banging out a groove on the massive wooden frame of the furniture. In a minute maybe he'd figure out a punch line and this mess would turn out to be nothing but a massive joke, with Maung waltzing in with more flowers. After all, Ne Win had resigned, supposedly retired over a month ago. So, that meant dictatorship was collapsing, the country was on the brink of democracy, all this chaos would be replaced with joy and prosperity any day. But they were living through a revolution, so of course people would be getting arrested, and they were all hoping it wouldn't be a bumpier ride than they'd expected.

For one thing, Wallace was confused about what really happened at the White Bridge. Rumors were going around of dozens killed, hundreds missing, but until now, he didn't believe it. In this political climate, reports get exaggerated. But obviously, some people were shot at. Maybe someone was killed. But in Burma, after you break the law, if you're smart, you go into hiding, and the mail service wasn't operating let alone the phone service, it was hard to know exactly what was really happening, or who was where. Wallace expected a little chaos. They'd all expected a little chaos. But it was starting to feel like too much chaos.

"They'll come around again tonight," Mya said. Wallace didn't like it when Mya whispered, and she was whispering all the time now. "We should get out."

Mere hours after their landlord visit, an "Officer Ywa," a skinny man in an overly large uniform, also knocked on their door. A big handgun strapped at his waist, he said he needed to see their papers, took their passports. He spoke English very well, but never had very much to say.

"No more traveling. You must stay at home for the next 72 hours"

"But we can go to the market? I need to go shopping."

"If you go to police station tomorrow, and bring your work permit, student permit, visas" he said, "perhaps they can help you."

"When can we have our passports back?" Gurney asked as he backed out the door.

He said, "You will have to ask them at the police station."

"Wait," Wallace said. "Bo Yaw, we can leave. We can go to Thailand, first thing tomorrow morning."

The officer's expression was icy. "Good luck," he said and hustled off as electricity and water service in their part of the city went dead.

"I think this is called letting the air out of Maung's tires," Wallace said. "We can't help Maung if we're busy trying to get our passports back at police headquarters."

"We can't stay here!" Gurney said, "They'll come back and throw us in the jail too! We have to contact the embassy or someone. We need a phone that works."

Mya said, "I always expected them to try to chase us all out."

"I'm not worried," Wallace said.

"General Than always envied us too much," Mya worried.

"That's probably true." The temperature was high enough on the roof to make the cistern water scalding hot. Mya washed the dishes, put them away.

Wallace said, "We could get arrested on the way to a phone."

"Well, I'm the only one who looks Burmese," Mya said, "I'm probably the best candidate to blaze a trail."

That's how they decided that Gurney's mother would go to Ting Hill monastery. It was the only place they knew of that usually had a working telephone. From there, she could make some phone calls, help organize their financial as well as physical escape, and wait while Gurney and Wallace would look for Maung. They planned for two days, right after the rallies, and then they'd all meet at Ting Hill, and drive to Thailand from there if it still seemed necessary.

By five o'clock, they'd packed the car, made their way to the bus station where everything was so coated with dust from the street that the air was barely breathable. It needed to rain. Teenagers toting machine guns were positioned at almost every intersection.

In the back seat, Gurney was taking pictures of soldiers through the open car window.

"They're a bunch of kids," Wallace snorted. He stopped the car, stroked his wife's arm, and looked back over his shoulder. They were in a good spot, behind a cement barrier, five steps from the bus. Mya stretched from the passenger seat over the stick shift, hugged him, and winked at Gurney. Gurney could see sweat on her father's neck, the lines in her mother's face. He was saying, "At least, we'll probably get some great photos out of this."

"You're being ridiculous," Mya said.

"I'm not thinking fortune. I'm thinking fame!"

Gurney pointed the camera at them. Wallace brushed his wife's bangs with his fingertips, kissed her forehead. "I love you," they said.

The flash worked.

"Insider photos, coffee table book, maybe sort of a scrapbook documenting the flowering of democracy in Asia,"

Wallace was joking hopelessly. "I'm thinking that'll be very cool."

Mya reached back, ruffled her daughter's hair. "Just stay in one piece and I'll be satisfied."

Mya's jasmine perfume, red lipstick and green silk long filled the car with a strange vigor for such a physically small person, but she had the strength of having already been a refugee once. Nothing surprised her. She wasn't a clingy person.

"Those cameras are wrecking your posture," Mya said, and Gurney un-wilted herself, tried to sit up straight, but then they were all bundling out of the car. Gurney snapped more images of the hugging and kissing goodbye.

"Don't waste film," her father said.

"Then don't smile like that," Gurney answered.

Everyone wanted to be told exactly what to do.

Mya got on the bus.

It wasn't until the bus left the city, rumbling past overloaded cars, boarded-up window, tired boy soldiers leaning against weapons like canes, not until the second it was too late that they all began to have doubts, and wished they'd stayed together.

3. Family Life Cambridge, Massachusetts. September 19, 1999

"Gurney, I love your cleavage," Bill Borrows said this in a tone of voice that was familiar to anyone who knew him. The fact that Gurney was sensitive, private, and somewhat shy was something Robert's boss liked to toy with. It was the same tone Borrows used when chatting with Robert at big business meetings. If he could embarrass someone and get away with it, Borrows enjoyed doing that. "Your skin is the color of milk."

"Owner's hitting on me," Gurney reported to her husband, for the second time that night.

The first time, Gurney's voice slurred, she being a lightweight for this sort of drinking, and Robert thought she'd said something about Borrows shitting on her.

And of course Borrows was hitting on her, the way her arms floated out of that black dress like a magic trick, that face, those eyes, it would be painful for a narcissist to even look at her. No one paid enough attention to Borrows when Gurney was in the room.

Bill's wife, Julia Borrows, was a very different sort of beauty than Gurney, more resilient, less fragile looking, muscular, curly haired, 100% round-eyed American. Robert enjoyed Julia's company and found her a refreshing aspect of this new organization—certainly more interesting than Bill Borrows. Bill could be such a jerk. Now Julia Borrows was standing by the buffet, eating grapes by the handful, shifting her immense bosom with a few tugs of her bra, talking loudly, gyrating slightly to the music being DJ'd by their most-reliable baby-sitter, Gurney's second cousin, Desmond. Desmond was watching Julia eat grapes and switching CDs with an expression of awe and amazement on his face.

Robert told himself to stop staring. He had his own delicate wife to think about, plus he valued his new job. It was the first good job he'd ever had, and Boston is an expensive place to live. It didn't seem likely he could blow it just by ogling the boss's wife, but one needs to be careful just the same.

A little vino splashed on the rug. Gurney was whispering to him again, "Robert, I mean it! Can't you keep him busy?" Her eyes were watering, and Robert couldn't believe an imbecile like Bill Borrows could make Gurney cry. He wanted to say, take the guy as the joke he is, but Borrows was standing right there.

So Robert kissed his wife where her hair made a little Z, gave her a friendly squeeze. Gurney pushed past them both, stumbled off into the kitchen.

"Thanks for your place, Robert. I didn't mind the meeting at M.I.T., but I wouldn't want to drink over there!" Borrows was in a cheerful mood. Robert took a sip of martini, but it wasn't easy to relax around the boss. The award he'd been given for his article published in Global Expansion Research News had been nice and Robert wanted to appear grateful, but he was tired and ready for bed. Before he could inject anything witty into the conversation his boss charged off into the kitchen, "Gurney's rice dumplings," he said. "Yum."

Julia was dancing Desmond across the living room rug, twirling, laughing loudly. Gurney came running back, and Robert took her hand. Sometimes Gurney and Robert danced amazingly well together, but not tonight. The music was wrong, and then Robert was dancing with Julia, and Gurney with Desmond, who put his arm around her shoulder and twirled her toward the kitchen again. It looked like she was crying.

Robert appreciated Desmond, his whole Buddhist thing, Free Burma thing, the way he cared for Gurney and their son as though they were his own, the way he could talk with Gurney about her parents, and understand what she was grieving. Desmond had helped Gurney's transition back to the real world, as Robert called it. So he didn't mind all the time they spent together. He just didn't want Gurney to fall apart and display any big emotions right now in front of his boss. Emotion only encouraged him.

Fortunately, Bill Borrows was on the stoop checking for messages on his cell phone, smoking.

So Robert put his hand on Julia's spine, into the small of her back, but the next song was Rolling Stones and Julia was more intent on burning calories than dancing. Robert was tired, and Julia was the perfect height where Robert could rest his chin on her head. Stumbling, he opened his eyes. The tweed of the rug was vibrating, and Julia was struggling to hold him up. Gurney was sitting on the sofa, watching Robert with a serious expression in her big eyes.

"The taxi's outside," she said.

It honked as though it heard her.

A cup of tea in his hand, Desmond smiled and said, "I called it for the Borrows'."

"Oh-ye-of-little-body-hair," Robert said, because they had this sort of relationship. Desmond drinks tea all day and all night. Desmond saves his teabags. Desmond the Do-gooder. Desmond and Robert sometimes annoyed each other. Especially when Robert was drunk.

Julia's hair had tangled in one of Robert's shirt buttons, and she couldn't unpin her head from his chest. Desmond and Gurney exchanged goodnight hugs while Robert helped Julia untangle.

"In solidarity," Desmond told Gurney, smiling, hi-fiving her.

Julia yanked her head and left a handful of curly gray and brown hairs pinned to Robert's chest. He pruned the hairs.

Gurney rolled her eyes. "Please. Everybody," and she smiled towards Julia, who was still rubbing her head. "Thanks so much for coming." She smiled at Bill Borrows. Her face had on a bright blank sleepy smile. Julia gave Robert a peck on the cheek, giggled, and waltzed out the door.

Borrows lurched up from where he was leaning and bumped into Desmond. "Sorry," Borrows said, then bumped into Robert, who was relieved to notice his boss was drunker than he was. "I drink more when I'm trying to quit smoking."

Desmond was last to leave.

"Not the best night to talk about the Burmese boycotts," Desmond said. "Sorry about that."

It was late. They were all exhausted, and couldn't tolerate more discussion, but when Robert got drunk he got argumentative. "No one paid you the slightest attention," Robert said. Robert finally found the crumb that had been in the corner of his mouth for half an hour, and wiped it off. He said, "I happen to like my job."

"I like my jobs too," Desmond said.

"All of them" Robert picked another long hair off his jacket.

Gurney rubbed her arms. "You don't need to apologize to me," she told Desmond.

"Apologize to me, then," Robert said.

Gurney said, "When I set aside the too cha and Bill took it and ate it, no one apologized to me."

Robert said, "Isn't it better for him to eat it, than to have it go to waste"

"Setting aside the first serving is not waste," Desmond said. "It's just little one scoop of rice. It's for remembering."

"Well Borrows isn't going to let me forget your shriek."

"Robert, I'm sorry. Maybe it seems like silly superstition, but that rice was supposed to honor my parents. And to have Borrows eat it! aaargh! I can't stand that guy!"

"Maybe Borrows will do something to honor to all our parents," Desmond said. "We have to give him a chance. He might change his point of view."

Robert said, "Or maybe he's cursed, and all his nose hair fall out."

"There is still hair on your jacket," Gurney said.

Desmond searched in his pockets for gum, unwrapped it, and folded it into his mouth. "Borrows is so rude," he said. "What a jerk. I couldn't stand it!"

"Oh Desmond," Gurney said, and kissed his cheek. "You were my hero tonight."

"You really can handle yourself around Republicans," Robert added. "I'm impressed. I'm sure it was difficult on many levels."

Gurney tottered down the steps in her heels, came back holding up a round packet of red and white checked paper in her hand.

"Cherry bomb, I think they call that one," Robert said. "Or is it a bottle rocket?" They all looked it over. "And I was just about to say how nice it was to have no blow-ups all evening."

Gurney explained, "Hill School took a firework out of Bobby's backpack last week, nearly expelled him for it. Jesus, I don't want him to be expelled."

"Don't be paranoid," Robert said. "This has been rained on. It's trash. Nothing to do with Bobby."

"You're not much of a worrier when you're drunk," Desmond said.

Robert played with the little bomb.

31

"Try asking about it without making a big deal." Desmond volunteered at Big Brothers Big Sisters, so they often had to indulge his opinions regarding Bobby. "He won't tell you anything if he thinks it'll get him into trouble."

Robert gestured with the cherry bomb, as though he might to throw it until Gurney took it out of his hand.

"It's probably completely innocent," Robert said.

"Bobby hates it when you drink," she said.

Desmond left.

Gurney lightly slapped Robert, "You brat. I wish you were my hero," then kissed his cheek. The house was quiet. Bobby still wasn't home. Generally he kept the radio on in his room 24/7, but tonight he ran in and out of the house party like it was a village with the plague. The house was unusually quiet.

The townhouse was positioned two streets behind Storrow Drive, where the city, the whole country was digital, modern, slick but old dirty technology was still making traffic, choking out soot, giving kids asthma. It seemed like a safe enough neighborhood. They had to climb steep risers, built in the 1800's, up from the street, then up, and up again in three narrow old-fashioned floors, with new stainless kitchen, the history and longevity of the house affecting the way they saw their lives, contributing to an inevitable sense of time and the thriving of art, education, culture, commerce. They'd bought in just in time.

Married life, like townhouses, plumbing, schools, roads, always requires some work. But Gurney and Robert compared their marriage to the rock of Gibraltar. Together they could get a lot done in a day.

Partly it was her relative youth. Things constantly rotting and needing replacement didn't bother her. She never expected light bulbs to all work or paint to stop peeling or pipes stop leaking. And the way toilets clog, doorknobs fall off, grout wears out, things get moldy - their house sometimes frustrated Robert, but never Gurney. Unlike Robert, she seemed to enjoy the handyman stuff; it didn't scare her that mundane thankless tasks can be a full-time job. Gurney whisked out meals and planned regular family trips to museums; she kept the house in good repair. Robert appreciated her practical abilities.

Gurney had a more difficult time dealing with red tape. It made her somewhat sick and discouraged to fill out pointless forms and to smile at incompetent nincompoops, which was exactly the sort of thing that didn't discourage Robert. In the early years of their marriage, they dedicated themselves to wading through quite a lot of red tape, pestering State department and Burmese refugee organizations and Red Cross and monasteries to search for any remains of her mother, father, or Maung. But the only measurable result was that their house was a toxic mess and the gutters clogged with leaves and record-breaking icicles, threatening them with head injuries from January to March. So about five year's earlier, they'd given up on that, it had just been too frustrating and exhausting for Gurney. They were intentionally making time to do other things.

So the party was cleaned up, Gurney was beside him on the living room couch, teeth brushed, eyes closed, chin lifted, stroking his head with one sleepy hand, holding a book open with the other. The house was cool and well organized. She moved her arm over her eyes, set down her book.

He stretched, knocked over the photo on a side table. It was a picture she'd taken of him asleep on a beach, five-week-old Bobby tucked under his arm.

She said, "I have nightmares every single night."

"Not every single night. You can't have nightmares when you don't sleep," Robert said.

Gurney looked up at the ceiling.

"Your eyelashes are so dark."

She turned away, but then surrendered slightly, cuddled into him. "Maybe one day I'll go take a shower and walk out a blond."

"Don't you dare." Robert leaned toward her and inhaled. She smelled like lavender soap. Eyes, ears, nose, mouth, fingertips, and Gurney: his sixth sense.

"You're perfect the way you are," he said. "Especially your boobs."

He pushed the afghan aside, wiggled in his legs and feet, and she flinched. He needed a shower. It was too much contrast - the crass aging klutziness of his body, the smooth young muscle of her arms, the sweet shape of her face. Lifting her sweatshirt, he cupped her belly. He stroked her. In spite of life's little challenges, being married to Gurney was nice.

The lamp was heating up his bald spot. He switched it off, clung precariously to the couch. Gurney sighed, flipped away, wedging her face between a cushion and the back of the sofa. Reaching behind her, she pulled at him, seemed to struggle with their positions. Then she threw his arms off her into the air. He fell onto the floor.

Teenagers were outside, yelling on the sidewalk— maybe Bobby getting home. They both looked up but the front door didn't open. A little cloud of cigarette smoke rose up from the street past their window. The room seemed to waver in the light.

Gurney said, "If he doesn't call or get home in the next two minutes, I'm never letting him to go to Janet's again." She thumped her chest.

"Try another ten minutes before you worry."

Robert adjusted a cushion, groped for his wife's belly, her soft breasts, like petting the belly of a cat, relaxing. She laughed, yielded, rolled under his touch, clearly wanting the same sort of relief he did.

They could hear the dishwasher going in the kitchen, their collection of clocks ticking. A fly buzzed by their heads, landed on the windowsill. "Worrying doesn't help," she agreed.

"Yeah," he said. It seemed like the right moment to mention this. "Like me. I worry. Like, I worry what you think when you think about Maung."

Gurney sat up. "That's really stupid. Don't say that Robert. That's not even funny." She climbed over him off the couch.

"Gurney, can you be fair with me? I just found that book, that's all. Was it you who left it out? Or was it Bobby?"

"Bobby has a right to be proud."

Robert was suddenly oddly, deeply upset. A train rumbled the house from two blocks away. "Proud? Proud about what?"

Gurney whispered, "Maung was a lot like you. You would have loved each other."

"We wouldn't have ever known each other. "

"He'd say the funniest things, like sitting in this cafe once, watching people walk by, and he whispered these funny erotic things across the table. Burmese men don't typically do that."

"Do you have to tell me this?" he said.

"Okay Robert, no, I can't even tell you this, I can't tell you anything because you are jealous of nothing."

He said, "I can't think of anything funny or erotic."

"Yes you can," she said.

His mind went completely blank.

"Go on," she said. "Anything."

Robert's train of thought was completely broken.

She sat with his lower body draped over her, his legs weighing her into the couch, and drew circles on his forehead with her finger, patted his legs. She said, "Maybe I should try calling Janet again."

"The platonic way you touch me sometimes really pisses me off," Robert said. "Nothing funny and erotic happening around here tonight, then," and he sighed louder than he expected. "Nothing like that grenade Maung had, swinging between his legs." Gurney pushed his legs off her lap, stomped out.

By the time Robert went after her, she was sitting on the toilet, the pink chub of her thighs covered with goose bumps, leggings around her ankles, blowing her nose. He stood in the doorway, trying to think of what he could say.

"I hate it when you watch me on the toilet," she said. "Go away!"

"I'm scared you don't like me."

"I do like you Robert."

"But I want you to love me," he said.

"I do love you," she said.

"You don't even have to love me," he amended, and meant it. "I just want you to lust me."

Her laughing and crying arrived together as usual. She sat up straighter, attacked the roll of toilet paper, spun it round, and then had to spin it backward. Robert stepped into the bathroom, took a stab at it, stopped the roll. She ripped off a handful of tissue.

"Look, you're not the only person in the world who's been traumatized," he said.

Gurney adjusted her clothes, stood up, and didn't look at him.

"For a person who doesn't believe in worrying, I never knew a worse worrier than you," he said, and wrapped his arms around her, kissed the top of her head. "Heck you worry about other nations. But I worry too. "

"We're as safe as anyone can be. Let's not dwell too much in the past," She said.

He kissed her head again. Gurney finished washing her hands and leaned against him again, wiping her face on his shirt. "I like it. Wipe away. Get those boogers all over me." He wasn't trying to be funny.

He led her into the bedroom (why couldn't she have led him"), pulled off his clothes to his underwear. They fell into bed, held hands. Voices carried up from the street below.

Putting his face on her belly, he said, "Concentrate on your breathing," and she seemed to relax. He listened, stroked her skin. All of her parts were so soft. Gurney started drumming her fingers on his head; a song he ought to know.

He tried again to think of a funny and arousing something. He wiggled his fingers into her armpit.

"Don't," she said, but he couldn't tell if she meant it.

"I'm ticklish."

"Your belly is making noises," he said.

"So's yours."

"I drank too much," he said.

"It was the chicken wings for me."

With the window half-open, cool air stroked across the room. Her finger drumming had a definite beat.

"Take Me Out to the Ballgame,'" Robert said.

"Wrong," she laughed.

Outside, someone swore in a loud kid's voice, and kicked over a trashcan.

"Is that... my... boy?" Gurney suddenly hissed. "Oomph! I've had it!" And she shoved off the bed, climbed over him to the bureau drawer.

"Don't," he said, "They're only kids." He didn't believe she'd light it.

"I can't help it," she found matches on the headboard; "I'm premenstrual." Usually she was good with kids.

"Don't," he said again, frozen, but she'd already struck the match, lit the firework and was watching the fuse burn with her lower lip thrust out.

"Toss it, toss it, God, that's dangerous!" he yelled, but she held it till the last possible moment, barely tossing it out the window as it exploded.

The bright blast left them deafened and seeing spots. A cloud of smoke, putrid sulfur, hovered in and against the house, so much smoke that it set off their smoke alarm. Every other neighbor on the street woke up while the kids yelled and scattered. The front door slammed open and shut. Bobby had been sitting on the front step the whole time. The smoke alarm shut off and a stereo came on in the bedroom below.

"Wow," she said, and then laughed, leaning back against the wall. "That was like, instinctual. I could write an advice column on how to get your kids into bed.'"

"I'm freaking out Gurney, I'm really freaking. I can't believe you did that. I can't believe it. God," he took a breath. "Your looks can be deceiving. You look delicate." Robert threw himself back into the pillows, almost crying with excitement, hating himself for falling apart, hating the way she must hate it.

"I'm not delicate." Her voice was soft again and she climbed back into the bed. "Really, you're the worst worrier in the family."

His heart pounded and he didn't want her to notice the vibration in his arms, so he rolled onto his back. Stumbling around, crawling over him, her breasts floated loose under the sweatshirt, hung briefly over his face. She weighed nothing.

A siren screamed in the distance. They heard adult voices, Ted calling in a dog, Rickie slamming his door. Then,

41

Robert couldn't stop himself from sobbing like a child. Next to her, he felt so weak.

She pulled at his shoulders, shaking him. She said, "Come on now. We could be the happiest people in the world."

She pulled her sweatshirt off over her head, kissed him.

Then she pulled off all her clothes, shook her nipples against his lips, spread her body across him like a satin blanket.

"See my funny nipples," she wiggled daringly, tried to make him laugh. "No crying allowed," she said, and kissed him again.

"Who are you to tell me what to do?" he asked, wiping leftover tears onto the sheet, kissing each perfect funny nipple. She chewed on his neck. He rose off the bed on hands and knees, and tossed her beneath him, excited. He did love his wife. Maybe she loved him too.

He was searching for something, and his fingers tested around. She moaned. It seemed so easy, suddenly, to be happy.

Rubbing against his thighs, she guided him, opening her legs, full of emotion. He held his breath.

A last gust of late summer air was pouring in through the window. They were drenched in sweat. He held her, kissed her face, her neck and shoulders, lost in sensations, shuddering.

A tapping noise interrupted them. Bobby was knocking at their door. "Mom? Dad? I'm home."

Gurney, sobbing, said, "I just want him to think. "

"That's all right," he told her. "Go on and cry. It's all right. Crying is good.

4. The Blade of Grass, Ting Hill Monastery. August 8-30, 1988

A week after Mya boarded the bus in Rangoon, Gurney's hair was disappearing from Mya's hairbrush, the scent of Wallace fading from her clothes. She tried to meditate, but instead went through arguments she wanted to have with Wallace when he finally got there, that General Than would kill them if he thought that would make someone more important happy, that it wasn't going to be easy to get out of Burma, at least not as easy as Wallace had always thought.

Peeling off her sweaty nightshirt, she washed herself with a cloth, a can of water, and nub of soap. A blade of grass lay curled on the window ledge.

The monastery had been built high on a hillside and there were gorgeous views of farm fields below. A slow trickle of water and a warm breeze ruffled the bougainvillea. Monkeys, birds, a little pack of dogs altogether were making a kind of music.

From an adjoining pagoda window, a young man leaned out, and his torso blocked sunlight entering her room and formed a slotted silhouette against her wall. Through window slats, she watched him pouring the water, rolling his young wet head in the sun, closing his eyes, and   Mya thought of Maung, and how the young boys seemed to be making such an effort to remain innocent.

Gurney would have jabbed her mother in the ribs, making a joke of it. "Come on Mumma. Let's shave our heads. It's cute!"

Not long ago, Burma seemed to be re-emerging as a democracy. Mya used to like the idea of Gurney marrying back into Burma, putting her education to work in the rebuilding of the country. But now she hoped more than anything that her daughter was headed back to the states. It was too dangerous here. But Maung would never let go of Burma, and it seemed unlikely that Gurney could ever let go of Maung.

"There are so many free countries, " Mya spoke out loud to the daughter who wasn't there, "how can anyone, in this day and age justify raising their family inside a dictatorship if they don't have to?"

When they were packing, Mya had told her that love can be complicated when politics are an issue, which was the kettle calling the pot black perhaps, but starting a family in Burma wouldn't be as easy as she imagined. Living in Burma for a few years is not the same as living there forever.

The young monk was still washing his head.

Before the University closed, Maung had boosted her confidence, playing the role of future son-in-law to the hilt, counseling as any good Buddhist would do to "Live in the present and worry about the future when we get there."

But of course you do have to think of the future. Even Maung, wrapped up in the poetry of this pro-democracy campaign, was all about the future. And children don't really understand how the world works. Hold onto ideals, but don't give up the simple pleasures! Mya didn't want Gurney to make useless sacrifices. If life can be easy, why not make it easy? Mya didn't believe in struggle for the sake of struggle.

The hot yellow sky and dusty air leaked between the full foliage of mango and breadfruit trees, glistening like satin against the monk's wet head. Raising the pitcher with one hand, he rubbed his head with the other, spit down onto the bushes, shook, and pulled himself back through the window. Several laughing voices resounded, and it seemed very strange to hear the young people laughing.

A trickle of sweat ran down her back. Chanting voices penetrated the walls, vibrating in low monotones, *Om, Mani, Padme, Hum.*

Mya dressed, tears rising and sliding down her throat, breathing deep breaths. She let the watery sound of her sandals slapping stone tiles between the nun's quarters and the central pagoda comfort her.

Over several days the artillery firing in the jungle had increased, and there were helicopters passing overhead, and black clouds underscored with orange sooty jungle fires scraping across the northern horizon.

People believe that evolution moves naturally towards self-government and democracy, but maybe evolution can move backward. Maybe there is no forward, no backward. She tried not to worry.

The next day, Mya wrote this note. "Master C gave me blade of grass to contemplate, and while contemplating I began to believe that the fighting line is between us, and you probably can't come to Ting Hill. I'm sending this to Nana's, in case you had to go back to Boston, to reassure you, not to worry. I'll meet you there, as soon as I can."

She wrote down their names, addressed the envelope to Boston, folded it inside her passport, and packed it into the lining of her suitcase. The next day, she moved the letter into a book she was reading. The fact that mail service wasn't available bothered her until she put it inside her dress shoes, added some currency, and stashed it all in a suitcase she could leave for them.

One morning, Mya paced the whitewashed hall and stairs through a louvered teakwood archway to the tiny monastery shop. The man who worked the shop had a middle-aged, fatherly face and cheeks that creased his smile. She pointed to a razorblade on the shelf over his head.

Rolling his hand across his scalp, his eyebrows rose, restraining laughter, yet miming the question, "You're going to shave your head?" Her ears burnt, and she shook her head, then she realized he was teasing. They both allowed themselves to laugh.

"There must be a Buddhist gene," Wallace had told her. "Picture me, shaved bald, in a robe." She remembered Wallace saying this, the weight of his body resting over hers in their bed, and she missed his weight, missed their bed. "I'm not that kind of guy," he said, but he could have been. Wallace told Gurney, "If I ever lose your mother, I'll become a monk."

"And if we lose you, Mommy will sneak around the border," Gurney had supposedly replied, "smoking and drinking and contracting malaria." Mya laughed. Mya laughed to herself, about how Gurney and Wallace were when they were together, and how they were probably having the adventure of their lives, and that it would be such a relief when they finally arrived.

But the monastery became increasingly crowded. Refugees, and little by little, arrived, and even with the quiet guarded like in a public library, or in a house where babies are sleeping, little by little it was getting noisier.

It took a lot of concentration to meditate in this situation. There was this fluttering feeling, but counting breaths helped to settle it down, and picturing a breeze bending softly across a field of rice, she did her best to entrain her thoughts, that helped her find some rest in the present moment even as she watched it recede endlessly away. Everything was okay. She expected them to show up any day. She prepared herself to enjoy a feeling of relief.

Clean water was being rationed off the cistern, so she tied her hair up, and waited for rain to collect a can of water, going barefoot down a stone path to the communal spigot. The day was quiet, with no sign of fighting yet this morning. Smooth, gray-green rocks shaded by enormous eucalyptus and smaller tropical fruits, plus a potted garden, exquisite topiaries and flowers were all arranged along the walking path. Everything was wet. A lizard stood rigidly in its tiny puddle, guarding a step stubbornly. Sloshing water, she stepped over it.

Where the terrace railing was carved into a snake, its golden scales coiling down the hillside, Mya lathered her hair,

49

and drenched herself. Cool rivulets ran down her cheek, snaked through the suds, and dispersed. Clouds split apart into a downpour, and she got the soap mostly out of her hair.

A week later, she sawed her hair off with a pocketknife. She washed and hung up her wet clothes to dry.

Mya contemplated the curled, dried remnant of grass near where a feral dog and her puppies were scuffling in the leaf litter. Then, Tat! Tat! Tat! Tat! Tat! She wasn't startled at first, but there was a rumble, and then again, the report of automatic rifle fire. Mya hurried down the hall.

Tat!Tat!Tat!

Men and boys who'd been filling the monastery all month were hurrying to look over the terrace walls. Dust was blowing up off the road. Mya's face trembled, and she tried to brace it with one hand, but the hand trembled too. Master C appeared and asked them to begin chanting. "*Gate gate para gate para sam gate, Bodhi, Svaha.* Gone, gone, all the way gone to the other side, to enlightenment."

The road and several canvas-shrouded vehicles were barely visible, obscured by roadside vegetation and ablaze in blinding sunlight. Mya shielded her eyes. A convoy of trucks had climbed through the cloud of dust, turned into the monastery drive, and come to a stop. The monastery's guests were streaming out the back doors, running for cover, into the jungle. Monkeys screamed like babies in the trees. Doors opened and slammed.

The woods, covered in a canopy of vines, were dim in contrast to the bright light of the terrace, and it took a moment for her eyes to adjust to it. A stick jabbed between the straps of her shoes.

Soldiers had streamed into the temple; she heard gunfire, and screaming.

A branch smacked into her face, she tasted blood, and like an animal she threw herself blindly forward until she fell, slicing open hands and knees and forehead on the way down a muddy embankment. A soldier was right behind her, pulling on her sleeve, kicking her like a stuck door, hitting her with the butt of a gun, and she was glad that Gurney and Wallace weren't there, relieved they didn't have to see this.

One of the soldiers shouted, excited, yelling, prying around her body, digging into her pockets, pulling at her clothes.

"Leave me alone," she suggested, smiling as it struck her, lying back in the water, that her family could never be apart.

The stream rolled steadily around her, a cool steady murmur in the quiet, colorless night, strands of hair swirling against her neck like river grass.

5. Narrow Escapes, Boston, Massachusetts. October 11, 1999

Gurney looked down while reaching up with a broom, thus nearly falling off the step stool where she was trying to knock leaves out from between the porch roof and the gutter.

"I'm surprised to see you here," she said, but seeing Bill Borrows on the brick sidewalk outside their Cambridge town home wasn't exactly a surprise. He'd been hinting, flirting with the idea of stopping by for weeks. He wanted to talk to her about something, and the air of mystery he put to it made her nervous. Sometimes, he said he wanted to look at her photographs. Other times he implied some sort of job offer was in the works. Other times, he left her thinking the only thing he was really interested in was seeing whether or not her could get in her pants.

Gurney's photography was hanging at the Cambridge Book Store. "I just saw your work hanging in Cambridge," he said. "You're an amazing photographer," then he repeated this over and over.

Gurney smiled, glanced across the street, up and down the row of townhouses. She asked, "Why aren't you working?"

"Meeting canceled. And the weather's so nice. I'm the play-hooky type."

53

"Bosses play hooky?"

"Absolutely. Why else would anyone want to be boss?"

Gurney hugged herself, rocked on her heels.

"What?" he asked.

"I didn't say anything."

A red Honda Civic bumped along the narrow street, then a black GMC, Bill Borrows scratched an itch. A striped yellow and red Town Taxi stopped a few doors away, honked.

Gurney's hair was blowing with the leaves, in all directions, blinding her in spite of the straw hat. Maybe dealing with Bill Borrows would be more interesting than unclogging gutters, maybe not.

On top of Bill's trim, well-exercised body his oddly small head was pitted against his large shoulders. Not a physically attractive man, but wealthy enough to be arrogant.

"You're too beautiful to be a witch," he said, gesturing to the broom.

She felt uncomfortably underdressed, and tugged at her shorts, crossed her arms over her belly. Gurney was dressed to take advantage of the last few rays of sunshine, not for a visit with Bill Borrows.

Fall foliage was at its peak. The Boston weather splashed sunshine one minute, and was painted in gray cold stone the next. Borrows grinned.

"I apologize for staring. I like the hat."

She patted the straw cone hat. Crumbs of it blew off. "It keeps dirt from falling in my face. I must look pretty silly."

"Not at all. Probably many Burmese tribal people wear cell-phones and carry brooms into rice-fields."

"At least a few," she answered, putting aside the broom and pushing off the hat, she grabbed her sweatshirt off the banister, dragged it on, rubbed goose flesh off her legs.

"You don't have to cover up for my sake," he said.

"I'm chilly," she said, brushing her long eyebrows back into place. "It's cold when the wind blows."

Her eyebrows swooped across her forehead like jewelry, like two smooth splashes of ink on white silk. Gurney was a rare bird in any part of the world, and Borrows was star struck.

A car rushed down the road, stopped outside the neighbor's door, tooted. Their daughter, Laura, came out wearing a tiny sundress, flip-flops and a sweater in her hands, hopped in the car and it sped away.

"You keep yourself busy," Borrows told her.

"I've never been good at sitting still, I'd never do well at a desk job. I need more physical stuff, like running," Gurney said. "I even run when I meditate. Maybe that doesn't look very Buddhist. But it helps me."

"I didn't realize you were Buddhist. Robert too?"

"Sorta."

"And you're raising Bobby as a Buddhist, too?"

"Bobby resists his parent's philosophy, like any kid." A yellow jacket buzzed and dived towards Borrows, who flinched. "He's a bit defiant. Like I was."

Borrows waved the insect away. "If Bobby weren't defiant, he'd be weird."

"You think so?" Gurney chewed her lip.

The clouds moved off, the wind died down, and it was hot again, sunshine blinding them, cooking them. He stroked out his tie, smoothed it over his chest.

"Teenagers are supposed to be defiant. Weren't you a defiant teenager? I'm hoping you can show me some more of your Burma photos." He puffed up a little, planted his feet even further apart, and peered past her into the house.

The screens in the open windows and doors wavered between shadows.

She hesitated. "But no one's home."

Borrows laughed. "You're home," he smiled. "Do you have coffee?"

"Coffee?" Gurney asked.

"Perfect," he said, and flipping his silly tie over one shoulder like a cartoon in a hurry, he marched right up the steps.

The kitty litter needed changing. Gurney felt guilty about every little mess, and guilty to be wasting time with Borrows when she could be doing something more useful. The grandfather clock chimed in its niche. She grabbed her portfolio. Maybe he really was going to buy a photo. She had sold quite a few, the blacks and whites and grays appealing to art collectors more for the way they looked charcoal drawings, than for the struggle for freedom she was trying to convey. She often remarked at how the context of her images never got through to people, but the absence of color did.

Borrows put on eyeglasses, spread out her work on the table. Gurney looked over his shoulder. There were lots of memories there: the temples, the elephants. That baby. None of the photos taken since then garnered as much interest.

"Yes," Borrows said, going slowly through the pile. "I have some clients interested in Myanmar. So that's why I thought you might have something I could hang something on my wall..."

"Burma," she said. "You mean Burma."

"It's the same place."

"The junta calls it Myanmar. The rightfully elected government calls it Burma." She went and got him a cup of coffee. "You have clients interested in Burma?"

He peeked at her over his bifocals. "The South East Asian frontier! I can't believe how perfect it is that you, of all people, and Robert are in the Borrows Inc. family now. That Robert has a "Burmese wife." He made quotes with his fingers.

"Well, I'm an American citizen, not Burmese. Lucky enough for me."

He lifted up a stack, wrinkled his forehead. "I appreciate the connection." He held up a shot she'd taken outside Ting Hill, smoke rising, the jungle dripping, with a smell of burnt hair still hanging in the air, when she'd closed her eyes, snapped the shutter. Borrows sifted through photos of burning and wounded and dead

She said, "That's later. On the border."

Bill Borrows set down the photos, put a hand on his chest.

"I feel a little bit sick," he said.

"Yes," she said.

Borrows went through the stack, seriously, silently.

"Gurney let me be straight with you. I should have told Robert this when I hired him. Borrows Inc. has relationships with various multinational companies, and some have lined up work with the development arm of the government of Myanmar. "

"Okay," Gurney said.

"That is our current state of affairs."

They stared at each other.

"So, what do you want me to say? Are you asking for my opinion?" Gurney asked. "No, I don't think it's safe to work with the junta that killed my family."

"Nothing is safe," he said, softening his voice, "What I'm wondering is if the Myanmar military has your name on a list? If they saw your name on a passport, if they'd stop you."

Gurney roared with laughter.

Borrows continued, ill at ease, "I'm saying, I might have reason, at some point, to send Robert to Myanmar. Robert, and you too."

Gurney sat on the end table, one hand still holding her coffee cup, looking directly into his eyes. She couldn't read him.

"Dictatorships are notoriously chaotic and disorganized, Mr. Borrows. They massacre their own taxpayers; I don't think it's an ideal atmosphere for doing business. Do you?"

Borrows waited a moment, as though letting that sink in, but then said, "Well, we have to think of the Myanmar of the future. Listen Gurney, I'm talking with you about this privately, rather than through Robert," Borrows said, and his body language shifted. He seemed more honest, but he hadn't made his point quite yet. "And I don't want Desmond brainwashing you either. He can be such a goody-goody pain-in-the-ass."

Gurney's eyebrows knitted together.

"I'm thinking about your old boyfriend too," he said, and at first, Gurney didn't understand who he was talking about. Borrows pursed his lips, and said, "Maung Naing is pretty well-known as a subversive. That could make you someone the junta would watch."

Gurney gasped. "Who told you about Maung Naing? And how dare you? I'm married. Maung Naing is not my boyfriend." She wanted to kill Robert.

Outside, another taxi started honking.

"I wasn't snooping," Borrows said. "Robert mentioned it."

For some reason her knees started knocking. Gurney clutched the edge of the counter.

"Take a breath Gurney and calm down." Borrows wiggled a finger in one ear. "Poet, freedom fighter, childhood sweethearts like that must have a big influence on people."

"I suppose they do." Gurney tried to make her voice sound casual, but it came out sounding strained. "But as a subversive, I'm ineffective to say the least. Somewhere in some tiny drawer the military might have scribbled down my name, but my name is Gurney White now, and I live in America, and my former boyfriend died about a decade ago."

"Don't Mr. Borrows me." He looked at her. "What makes you think Maung's dead?"

Gurney shrugged. "If he was alive, I would have heard from him. He would have contacted me." But the expression on Bill's face shook her. Gurney pushed the cat away with her foot. "Or maybe not. Maybe he wouldn't have. What do I know? The last time I spoke to him was 1988."

"Yes," Borrows said, and he picked up a photograph, one of the babies, a perfect Karen tribe baby, not a blemish visible on her silky skin—tiny hands, pearly nails, wrapped in embroidered silk, decked in orchids, wild flowers, herbs. He said, "A decade isn't that long. Maybe you just lost track of each other. "

61

When Gurney captured the image, the mother was carrying her baby's body, all decked out in silk and flowers, till they could bury it. The kitchen clock ticked loudly, the refrigerator switched on.

"I'd love to buy a print of this one," Borrows said.

She brushed the hair out of her face and said, "Fine. I'll make a print for you."

"Good!" he said, and clapped his hands like a movie director. "Can you walk me back to my office? It's not far. I left the checkbook over there. I'll pay you for the print. And I have something there I want to show you." Declining wasn't an option.

"Don't forget your camera," he said. "You should be out taking photos on a day like this."

She tripped on a brick popping up out of the sidewalk.

"You're not mad at me?" he asked.

"Why would I be mad?" She was thinking, if Maung was alive, he's married, a parent by now, as was she.

"Because I don't think Aung San Suu Kyi's way is the only way. Purity and ideals are nice, but she can't do things that we can do," he said, and he didn't smile. "She has limited options. On the other hand, we can go, get something accomplished, and get out."

"That's wishful thinking," she said.

"Look at you blush!" he said. "Why you did have an Irish daddy, didn't you. I'm not all bad Gurney. Trust me."

They ignored each other for a city block. Finally Borrows said, "It's not ideologues who are going to save the world, it's the entrepreneurs, companies like mine, people like us."

"Can you be both an ideologue and an entrepreneur?" she asked.

Bill squeezed his lips together, took the question seriously and said, "Depends on what you mean by ideologue. Everyone has a philosophy to justify what they do. I think a natural gas partnership is about development and education, and training workers and investing capital, and yes I am an ideologue as well as entrepreneur. But other people might not see it that way. "

They crossed a four-lane street with Borrows gesturing so much, she worried he'd get hit by a car. "Thailand as you know is the sex tourist capital of the world, the prostitutes see themselves as ideologues and entrepreneurs. Everyone sees themselves as an idealist. I'll tell you the kind of idealist I am, If I were ever to buy a prostitute," he confessed as they walked, "and of course I would never ever even consider for one small instant buying a prostitute, but if I did, I'd want to find a woman just like you. Your husband is one lucky man." As they got to the sidewalk, he took her elbow and actually leaned to whisper in her ear.

"Back the fuck off," she said.

"Oops, sorry, was that too intimate?"

"I don't know what you think about Asian women," Gurney fumed, "but that's not me."

"Since when were you an Asian woman? You didn't just lose Maung, you lost yourself."

The morning fog burned off the Charles River. There was a breeze. Gurney walked faster, running out of breath.

"Think coffee table book," he said. "Shoot for the moon."

"My Dad used to say that."

"Oh God, not that!"

Striding up a street she'd never seen before, with delightfully old brick houses, and a renovated little depot, he said, "Slow down, look around. My office is on this block. Isn't this cool?" It appeared once to have been some kind of an outpost where horses were kept, but it disappeared as the city grew up around it.

"This is my personal office, I have another over at Borrows Inc." He waggled his thumbs in his ears. "And you better not act shocked when I show you stash of 100% natural opium."

"Hahaha. I don't get it. You're telling me a joke. Right?"

"Guess," he said.

She said, "I can't guess. I don't want to guess."

"Oh come on. You do coffee don't you? You drink wine? Opium is safer. Don't pull the Madonna stuff on me. I know you better than you realize." He fiddled with the key to the old-fashioned door lock, "Like anything else, it's all in how you use it, it's not something I'd do every day, and that's why I wanted to share this moment with someone who'd appreciate it. Gurney, it's just not a big deal to me. But I know."

For the second time today, she wanted to strangle Robert. He tells Bill Borrows stories that are none of his business. Why? Were they drinking? Was this a guy thing? .

Borrows went to work on the finicky lock. "Not the refined chemical, that would be heroin, of course, that's not good, not good at all, but opium resin," he said, wiggling the key, "tribes people even give it to their babies, for teething, right. It's that mild. And this is my way of introducing you to something, totally not what you think, legitimate organizations doing research. Drug companies, big and small." Borrows' eyes twinkled at her. "Really. They need to have some opium to work with."

65

Gurney walked clasping her chin in her hands, shivering cold as she reluctantly followed Borrows through a door into a smelly exterior stairway covered with tarry aluminum siding over creosote, all permeated with cat piss. He took her elbow again. "But this is proprietary information. So don't mention it to anyone. Ha!"

"Stop playing with me," she said, shaking him off, and he led her up the stairs, clumping through twisted squares of sunlight blazing at the landing of each floor.

"This was an old fire station," he said, "It looks crappy out here, but wait till you see the interior." He pushed open the last door, dark oak in five panels and flipped on a light switch to a spacious room with high wooden ceilings, stained glass windows.

It was like walking onto the set of a movie, red satin draperies, a cast iron fireplace set into a tremendous sculptured marble hearth, leather furniture, oil paintings of schooners in frothing seas.

"That's a working fireplace, by the way. Not that we'd want it on a day like today, but maybe if you visit me here next January, or something." He smiled, winked. "I use it all the time. I love it. Oh, I see you like my crystal ball?"

"It's enormous," she said, and those candlesticks are impressive as well." They were cast iron phalluses, with bullrings in the testicular base.

"I was a teenage Goth," he said, and laughed. "I still am, at heart.

Gurney said. "It's a very nice fancy haunted house. " The nice weather of the day was sealed out completely. "Congratulations."

Bill went across the room, got comfortable on a leather couch while Gurney hesitated, and finally perched on the ottoman. She said, "Tell me what I don't know about Maung." That Borrows might know anything at all about him made her spine tingle.

Bill struggled for a moment with the couch pillows before he spoke.

"Gurney," he said, "I'm wondering if maybe we could help each other out here."

"Go for it."

"We can help Maung Naing. He's alive," Borrows said. "I know he is."

The hair on the back of her neck crept up. Gurney bent her elbows towards her stomach, braced herself, pressed against her eyes with her fingertips.

Bill opened the tabletop, pulled out a small teak box. "And this is a formula that funds some Burmese freedom fighters," he said. He packed the bowl of a water pipe.

Gurney nearly slapped him. "How dare you say that?"

"Some members of a little militia on the Burma/Thailand border need to raise money. Desperately. They have no food, no medicine, nothing to defend them. They're desperate people Gurney, do you know what it means to be desperate? So I have connections as you know in Burma, and they approach some of my connections, to make a deal with the only guys for hundreds if not thousands of miles around who have any money. And guess what we're buying. Life is not perfect. Nothing is perfect."

"He wouldn't sell out Burma that way."

"You think that's selling out? Really? Let's go through the options. You can continue to clean up after a brutal junta, which thinks nothing of burning out a village, enslaving the children, raping the women and killing the men, you can keep removing mines while they keep adding them, or you can win the war. Just do whatever it takes to put the fucking assholes out of business. This is an area of high conflict. This is an awful lot of trust on my part Gurney. Everything is out on the table."

Gurney gasped. "Are you kidding me? If the Myanmar military found out about this, we'd be assassinated over there."

"Well, we don't deal with anyone who doesn't really understand our language. We want clarity."

"That doesn't sound easy."

"It is easy. We just ask these guys for a personal English speaking reference."

"You're kidding."

"No, it must be an English speaker. All the references must speak English, and the better they speak English, the easier we figure it will be to work with you. When you learn a language, it's not just words, but culture, Gurney. You make a good connection, and that's how we know this guy isn't going to kill us in our sleep, and it's tough to find these people, usually it's someone with a personal reference. An exiled half-Burmese stands an excellent chance of getting our attention, like someone with an English Dad and a Burmese Mom. And guess what. Your name came up. You were used as a reference." The sweet scent of opium rose in the air. " Try this," he said. "It's actually very mild. Natural. You'll like it."

"Maung doesn't sell opium," Gurney said, "It's emergency medicine, to treat pain."

Borrows said, inhaling, "That's exactly how I use it. Come on. I thought this would be special. You must have some pain somewhere you'd like to get rid of. I sure as hell do. This helps my back." He stretched out his back, and put down the water pipe. "It's fine with me though. Do what you want. Don't smoke it if you don't want to. I don't mean to push it on you, I'm trying to be nice."

Gurney stood, turned around in a circle, sat back down, sighed. She needed to hear Borrows' every word. Anything is better than nothing.

"Okay tell me. Go ahead," she said. "Tell me the whole story."

6. What Happened to Her Father Rangoon, Burma August 8, 1988

All your life, you want to be needed, but then when it happens, it scares you to death. You need to smoke when you've got a beautiful young daughter in a dangerous world like this.

Wallace waved up at Mya on the bus, and slung the other arm slung around his daughter as the bus drove Mya away.

"Daddy," Gurney turned and kissed him on the cheek. "You don't even want to be here."

"Not true. This is one heck of an adventure."

"Thank you Daddy. Thank you so much." They spent most of the day on foot, winding their way between street vendors, looking for anyone who might have heard anything about Maung. People were very happy to see Westerners on the street. Every possibility was floating over Rangoon's filthy air and dense traffic.

"You need gills here," she said.

"Yeah," he said. "The air is so thick, I practically need to chew it."

They kept a cloth sprinkled with bleach-water in a sandwich bag, and after Wallace wiped down the lens of the camera with it, he passed the camera to Gurney. She squatted in the shade, focused on a banana vendor.

With classes canceled, and the entire city closed, if Maung hadn't been missing it might have felt like a holiday. There was a general strike. The airport was closed. Any citizens with money and power were gone. But the streets weren't empty, Rangoon didn't feel sleepy, and everywhere you looked, someone was selling food or flags. The sidewalk had become a carnival and the market closed with many new vendors taking its place. Buses entered the city so packed their doors couldn't close, pro-democracy banners and matching white armbands streamed out windows. The strength of the movement was impressive, inspiring, reassuring.

Gurney took a picture of her father's smiling face.

"Don't waste film on me," he said.

"Daddy, I'm trying to look like a tourist." She talked to her father from behind the camera. "And FYI, in the frame right behind you, a soldier's pointing his gun at us." She snapped the shot, looked up, smiled at him. "That was an amazing shot!"

They were on a public street corner, at the edge of the market. He turned around.

An acne covered teen, dirty hair squashed into his helmet, was glaring at them, holding onto an AK-47, and shifting the nozzle of the weapon back and forth.

"Freudian," Gurney said.

"Yeah, it's a big one," Wallace said, "So let's not be reckless, warrior boy is pointing his thingy right at you."

Wallace hardly dared break his gaze with the soldier kid but Gurney was giggling. She crinkled her eyes, addressed the soldier shyly. "I'm sorry. I don't understand. I am American," and she waggled her expressive eyebrows up and down, and that's all it took for soldier kid to shake his head, and visibly relax.

"Come," soldier kid gestured.

"Kiss the film goodbye," Wallace said.

Wallace had bought her numerous cameras, since lost to fires, car accidents, floods. What attracted her most was danger or destruction, and that was rough on cameras, but he loved what photography did for her, loved how it brought out her fearlessness like this, loved it, and it terrified him now as with only the slightest tremble in the corner of her smile, Gurney was walking towards soldier kid, focused on him as though he were a guard outside Buckingham Palace.

"Let's not be too silly, honey," he said. "Or he'll take the camera too."

A group of seven or eight-year-old girls were on the street corner, and were acting as though they'd never seen foreigners before, and Gurney looked like foreigner no matter where in the world she went. Having an audience frustrated the young soldier, and his acne-covered face turned red. Gurney brought the camera down to her belly, bowed apologetically as he swung the gun on his shoulder and gestured to Gurney for the camera.

As though out of habit but it wasn't, Wallace reached for his wallet and took out a fistful of bills, passed it to the soldier, who took the wad. A child ran up from the little audience, and Wallace handed her a fistful, too. "Easy come, easy go," he said, "money makes everybody happy." The soldier ignored her, and she ran off, shrieking in laughter to her friends.

Wallace kept frisking his own shirt as though he would endlessly find more wads of cash, though this was his last handful and his knees were shaking. The soldier stuffed the bills in his pocket, and turned to face an approaching car. Gurney pulled Wallace half a dozen steps off the road into a long alley full of dumpsters that squeezed into another street. They ran.

"Is that him shouting?" Wallace asked, puffing for breath.

"I think so," she said. They moved as fast as they could.

Behind the European-styled granite buildings smaller brick buildings, then shabby wood, then rows of corrugated cardboard and corrugated metal shacks, piled on top of one another. Gutters full of sewage dissected yards stinking and buzzing with insects and rats and rusty cans and empty bottles. Ginger root, and a scrawny plantain, grew up here and there; some growing as weeds and others in tiny tended gardens. Gurney tied back her hair, and put a scarf over her neck, as the mosquitoes were bad. Gurney and Wallace picked their way between ghetto kitchens and bedrooms and bathrooms, under flapping laundry, around cook fires, in mud under rickety stilted houses, over soapy puddles and patches of cucumber vine, over, under and between fragile buildings creaking with dogs and chickens and children. Finally they saw the main road.

He slapped away a mosquito.

Ahead, on the highway, a convoy of trucks, buses, and four armored tanks had stopped, facing east, engines humming. "Now that's a waste of the taxpayers' money," Wallace said.

Facing this barricade, a ragtag foot crowd of students, monks, drummers, dancers, children, parents, and grandparents appeared to have some sort of festival going, with banners and flags, even a clown and flamethrower. People were singing, drumming, making music.

"There's Trin, and Beado Win." Gurney recognized several students. "I don't see Maung."

"I'm exhausted," Wallace panted. "I'm getting too old for this."

"Me too," Gurney said.

He pulled back her scarf, stopped her to look in her eyes. "You okay?" She answered, "No. I'm scared. " So he took her hand and squeezed it. He said, "Let's take a break and come back. We haven't eaten anything since breakfast."

Swarms of students continued to pour onto the streets. Blocked in one direction, foot marchers found themselves blocked in another direction as well. They were being prevented from reaching City Hall. Long rows of stopped buses, scooters and bicycles lined the street.

Trin and Beado told them, "Officer Miyato told us Maung was released, but no one has seen him yet." They drove Gurney and Wallace the long way around the city center and dropped them near their apartment, to wash up and rest before demonstration speeches started, and in case Maung might be hoping to meet them there.

Wallace climbed the fire escape and shot footage of the local crowd. They ate, packed a few more essentials, washed hands and faces, changed clothes, drank water. They waited, while outside the crowd got louder. No one else seemed to be in the building.

Wallace told his daughter. "We can get take the car and drive out of town for the night, once the tanks move out of the way."

Then Gurney found the note Maung had left in their mailbox. "It says 'Go to Professor Hyim's.' "

Vendors were selling balls of hot rice, candy, box drink, banners, kites, torches. A merchant with a long, skinny braid rolled up yards of fabric, boarded shut his shop. People were hurrying around with water, food, fuel, and the overcrowding was starting to feel stressful.

The August sun began to set at 6 pm. There hadn't been much of an afternoon shower. Gurney wiped mold off the camera lenses.

A group of monks floated past, bowing, prostrating themselves against the ground. They rose altogether, and chanted. Folding their hands, they walked a few steps, bowed, and prostrated themselves again.

"I wish I was a monk," Wallace said.

"I know you do, Daddy."

The tremble gathered under their feet again. Tanks were moving in the city center, and Wallace's neck had a muscle spasm. A man walking behind them picked up money that had been dropped on the ground then threw it back down.

They passed a thin woman chewing, gesturing with a cricket's body between two fingers, delicately breaking off a leg, biting into the body, picking between her teeth. They wove around small abandoned piles of fruit and rags, to an open-air noodle vendor. "I'm so tired," Gurney sighed, and slumped onto the low stool. Wallace took the only other stool with a sigh, smoke curling up Wallace's cigarette hand like a pet snake.

"Rest," the noodle vendor said. "And be careful tonight. I wouldn't take photographs, not if I was either one of you."

"What do you mean," Wallace said. "They're only photos."

"Don't be an idiot," he said. "You could be shot."

Gurney and Wallace ate the noodles. "Such bad timing," he groaned. He lay down on the bench. Gurney looked him over. "I'm not having a heart attack, don't look at me like that. I just have an upset stomach. I need to use a commode."

"Daddy, I'll be right back," Gurney said. "You go ahead and use the toilet. I have to run to the hospital, grab the film I left there."

"Okay. Go ahead, I'm fine really, the regular food poisoning, nothing serious." They were right around the corner from the hospital, and she was gone about five minutes, when Wallace thought, that was a stupid mistake. He lit a cigarette. Another half hour, Wallace still was waiting for Gurney. He was just preparing to go look for her when the shooting began.

It started at some distance, sounding like a roar of applause, but then became an approaching cacophony, and as the roar got closer, and you could tell it was shooting, screaming.

People were running. In the sky, a smoky urban silhouette was still lingering, like thick black ink. A hornet whistled past his ear. "Bullets," someone said. He ducked. Soldiers were coming up the street.

At first, no one could believe it, hunkering down as they ran, aiming for things like cars, the corners of buildings, they ran crouched, and dropping into a doorway, and there was boy about Gurney's age, trembling, shaking the door to the building, cursing. The soldiers got closer, and the boy burst off, knocking into a woman who fell on the street.

You could smell blood. Tanks, and soldiers shooting guns were right there, right in front of him, and they were shooting people with armbands. Wounded people were in doorways, on the sidewalks and Wallace expected to be shot.

Then foot soldiers came around the corner too, and a girl crashed into him, blood spouting from her leg, and she ran clinging to Wallace for several steps, then a new crowd surged around him, tearing away their armbands desperately, and people were getting shot. It amazed him, as the crowd fell and thinned, to find his own body unharmed, hurrying across the road, and he thought he saw Mya, then Maung, then Gurney and a light-skinned body was on the ground, and Wallace touched it, nearly collapsing. But it wasn't Gurney, and he kept going.

It seemed like it took him forever to get to the hospital, and several bodies in white hospital uniforms were sprawled, dead, across the steps. Wallace couldn't believe it. It looked like a group of doctors. *They're shooting doctors?* And there, draping sheets over their bodies was Gurney. She shouted at him, "Daddy!"

He ran to meet her, and dragged her back across the street and didn't realize he was hurting her until she screamed.

Bodies, collapsed canopies, abandoned vehicles were here, and they were behind the soldiers, behind people left standing with bullet holes like miniature volcanoes, losing strength in a lava flow of blood.

Gurney shivered against the back of his knees. Wallace whispered, reaching one hand to his daughter, took her elbow, led her at a crouch deeper into the back street alley. They both heaved with nausea.

"There, now we feel better." He wiped his mouth, tried to sound calm. "Professor Hyim's apartment," he said. "He's got the transmitting drum."

"We'd have to cross that road," she said.

He took her elbow, shook her. "It's officially your turn to be brave," he said, but she blubbered like a baby.

Wallace took a breath, pushing away a feeling of vertigo, more startled by his daughter's pale face than by the sudden sight of his own blood filling his shoes. Gurney was looking at his shoes. "What's that?" she was asking.

"Noodle soup," he said. The night air was darker, the color of blood. "Almost as good coming up as it was going down."

"Your shoes," she said.

"I stepped in something."

Someone was running towards them, so Wallace pulled Gurney deeper into the alley, never so happy to find trashcans. There was a door, but it was locked.

81

He said, "This could make a good documentary." Flies swarmed around them, clung to their faces.

"I hate documentaries," Gurney said.

They giggled together, shivering.

"We're so lucky," Wallace said. "How'd we get out of that?"

"Daddy, are you bleeding?"

"That's okay," he said, "I'll just keep pressure on it."

A car sped by, lights bumping holes into the dark. They leaned trembling against the building. "See that door?" They were across the street from an indoor market, a mini mall. The door was partly open. He stuffed exposed film into her pockets.

A major chord, of a jeep, helicopter, generator, and barking dogs sounded. "When I say run," He said, using his most fatherly tone, "Run. I'll meet you there. Understand?"

He smiled, held her, tried not to wobble.

She said, "I love you Daddy."

"I'll be right along," he said. "Run."

She jogged across the road to the marketplace, hesitating at the entrance. A shadow moved across the display windows. People were inside the door. Gurney whirled and tripped back to the sidewalk, and down the side of the building. "Run! Daddy! Run! Jesus! They're going to shoot!"

He didn't weep; he wasn't even worried, he just shouted, "run!" And when the boys in uniform staggered out of the market, they heard Gurney's footsteps first and looked in her direction. Wallace called them, "Hey!" He held up the empty camera by pure instinct. "Hey! Hey! Hey!"

Gurney was halfway down the sidewalk. The soldiers lifted their weapons like this was a game, like kids do when they're playing. Then one kid nudged another, and they all turned towards him. Wallace held up the empty camera his arms shaking, and a bullet flew over his head. It surprised him. "You don't need to do that," he said. "I surrender." The soldiers clumped together.

And Wallace felt thankful Gurney was gone, but she was looking back. She saw her father pose, saw his arms go up, the camera come flying out of his hands. She saw the soldiers killing him, and she ran.

7. Dealers. Boston, October 12, 1999

Gurney was sitting at the kitchen table reading aloud while Robert leaned against the counter, the belt buckle Bobby gave him for Father's Day digging into his waist, and tried to pour coffee without letting Gurney see his hands shake.

"Okay," he said, "I'm stumped. Why was the scuba diver found dead in the forest?"

"Helicopters scoop 20,000 gallon buckets of ocean water to dump on the fires," Gurney read, and looked up. "The diver was swimming where the helicopters were scooping."

Robert had shaved and slicked his hair back. He was wearing a tie with a painting of a peacock that Gurney had given him the previous Christmas, while Gurney was still in her robe, a wreck. Her hair was dirty; she tired, older than her usual 33-year-old look.

"I know what I would've done," Robert said, "if it'd been me."

"Helped smother a fire?"

"No, swim to the top of the bucket, and bang."

"Anyone see my cleats?" Bobby was stomping around, making lunch while eating breakfast.

"I thought soccer was over," Gurney said.

"No," Bobby and Robert answered in unison. "One more game."

The jar of mustard splashed on the floor.

Gurney asked Robert. "You think you're immortal?"

They kept a box by the entryway for sports equipment, and Gurney commenced to dig through that. "No one would have heard you," she told him.

"Does mustard stain?" Bobby was asking.

Robert engaged the conversation as though it was tennis. He loved batting ideas back and forth with Gurney. "There's nothing wrong with optimistic thoughts. As they dump the bucket, I make my famous tuck and roll landing."

"That the same thing this guy did."

On the sidewalk outside their home, children in bright plaid uniforms, like small battalions of fast-food vendors, headed to school. The approach of winter felt remote enough to be exciting.

"Bobby, you don't need to act so angry all the time," his mother said.

"I'm not angry," he said.

"Then I just don't understand. You're a good student. Don't you want to go to school? You're late almost every day."

"Arghh!" Bobby groaned, wiping a sponge across his shirt.

Bill Borrows told Robert recently, "all kids need a kick in the pants sometimes." Robert looked at Bobby pulling himself out of his shirt and noticed how incredibly he resembled his mother. Fragile looking out the outside, tough as nails on the inside, and in Robert's opinion, there was no need for any pants kicking. "He just spilled the mustard," Robert said.

"What are you doing in school today?" Gurney asked him.

"Nothing," Bobby said, and ran his shirt under the sink. Gurney raised her eyebrows.

"We never do anything," he said, "except listen to teachers talk."

"Computers?" Robert asked him. "I thought you were doing a computer class."

"Yeah," he said. "But I already know all that stuff."

One of the three therapists they'd visited recommended giving Bobby more space. Their idea was that he needed to 'differentiate,' to test out his growing independence, to be himself and not his parents. And that was an issue. Who he was, and who his parents are. The other two councilors said all teens are like that, and there was nothing to worry about, but Gurney was the one who needed something, to develop some outside interests, to get a life that went beyond her internal life; but what her internal life was, or whether it was such a good idea to bring it to the surface, Robert wasn't sure. Gurney wasn't sure either.

Robert watched her leaning on her elbows on the table, new dark circles around her eyes. "Are you okay?" he asked.

"I've got my period," she said. With a role of paper towels, she mopped up mustard.

"Man," Robert said. "That was a full jar."

"I know," Bobby said. "That's what I'm saying. This is the first time I've worn this shirt!"

Robert fiddled with the computer laptop on the kitchen counter. Scanned the day's headlines. "Bangkok Post says eighteen Americans have been arrested in Myanmar."

She said, "For what?"

"Protesting," Robert said. He skimmed ahead.

"Robert you are annoying me to death today."

"Will you please not fight in front of me?" Bobby asked. Robert gave up the computer to pour another coffee. He wasn't so much worrying about whether it was the alcohol, or if he was developing Parkinson's or a blood sugar problem, or overstressed at work, but he didn't want Gurney to see his shakes.

She told Bobby, "Toss it in the wash sweetheart."

Bobby left the room, crying, "My Sox shirt!!" and Gurney turned to Robert.

"Caffeine gives me jitters," he said. "Weird. Do you see how my hand is shaking?" He held out a hand.

"Weird." She glanced up. "So what is that story?" she asked him.

"You can read it," he said. "I left it on the screen."

Gurney read it out loud. "Authorities in Burma/Myanmar are pondering what to do with 18 foreign political activists. Detained for handing out leaflets expressing support for democracy and human rights, they were urging remembrance of the suppressed democracy uprising of 1988."

Robert wiped crumbs off the counter. "There's an itinerary, for you; find a dictatorship, stage a protest. Someone was drunk when they thought up that idea."

The timer buzzed; ten minutes till blast off.

Gurney was putting dishes in the sink, so he had to hug her from behind; and while he was reaching around, he squeezed her breasts. She squirmed uncomfortably.

"Sore?"

"I told you, I've got my period."

"I'm such an idiot," he said. "What can I do that would feel good?"

She rinsed out a milk jug. "Make me Queen of Everything."

"No can do. But stick with me kid, and I'll make you Queen of Borrows Incorporated," he said, and took the carton out of her hands, tossing it into the recycle bin.

"Ugh!" she said, rolling her eyes in disgust.

He went on, "I'm not supposed to blame your period, though, right?"

Her eyes were swollen.

"Are you getting sick?" he asked her.

"I don't think so," she said, and turned towards him.

Tears rolled over her lower lids.

Robert said, "You certainly do have your period," and he spread open his arms. "Here. Get a totem pole hug. It's not just from me, but from the bird on my tie and the bull on my belt." His hands started to shake, but he controlled it.

"I'm sorry," she said, and embraced him.

"I'm sorry too," he told her.

Bobby came back into the kitchen wearing a new shirt, picked up his book-bag, stretched the straps over his shoulders. They wouldn't see Bobby again till supper.

Gurney went to get aspirin.

"What would you do if you were King of Everywhere?" Robert went for a question requiring more than a yes or no answer.

Bobby said, "Execute all the annoying people."

"Great." Robert said.

Bobby leaned against the table, stretched his narrow neck, the downy hairs there angled to meet his spine and thin, catlike shoulders. "But I don't want to be King of Anywhere," Bobby said.

"Fortunately," said Robert.

"Kings are pains in the asses," Bobby said.

"Buttocks," Robert corrected.

"What do you want to do when you grow up, then?" Gurney asked. "Really Bobby, I'm curious. " Usually she was smart enough to avoid this sort of conversation, because Bobby hated this sort of conversation.

But now, he contemplated, then said, "Buy pizza, rent videos."

It was Tuesday. The trash truck was coming up the road.

"If you're not careful you'll wind up driving a trash truck," Gurney said.

Robert added cheerfully, "that's better than smuggling drugs, or becoming a pimp." Their wristwatch alarms started to go off, and Bobby gave his mother a kiss on the cheek. "I love you Mom."

"Love you, too," she told him.

Bobby said, "I love you Dad." Gave his father a kiss.

"What time will you be home?"

"This is my last night of detention. Remember?"

Bobby's pants were hanging around his hips, but he'd never pull them up if you asked.

"How could we forget?" Robert said, but he'd forgotten all about the detention. In his peripheral vision, Robert caught Bobby hiking up his pants.

"So, five o'clock," Bobby said.

"Think homework. Get something done while you're there " Robert told him. And to Gurney he said, "He sat up all last night making that poster."

"Really? Way to go Bobby. It looks great."

"You were so zonked last night," Robert told her. "I couldn't believe how early you went to bed. Otherwise I would have showed it to you."

"I had a busy day," she said. "I was beat. Bobby, what is this poster supposed to be?"

"See Dad? I'm not bringing it in. It's too weird."

"What do you mean," he said. "It's the political parties, I see the elephant and the donkey."

91

"Oh," Gurney said. "Now I get it."

"But this isn't what Mr. Hunt wanted. I screwed it up. I'll bring it in late."

"Don't bring it in late," Gurney said.

Robert put a hand on her arm.

Bobby called "Bye!" and ran out.

Then Robert dropped his cup in the sink and broke it, got caught on up a bracket by the door and ripped his jacket lining, and as he bent to kiss her, she turned away. Her face looked wobbly. She said, "Call in sick." He tucked in his shirt; she touched the bird.

"Don't flirt," he said, smoothed the ends of the wings together. "I wish I could stay here and take care of you every time you got your period. But I don't want to lose my job."

"Why?" she asked. "What's so great about your stupid job?"

"I don't have to punch in a clock. I have a nice office. I make a pile of money," he told her, and it was true. "This is the best job I've ever had in my life." He'd never expected to earn income like this. "I don't mind going to work at all."

They were in the hall in front of one of her favorite photographs: her mother and father at the Ting Hill monastery.

"I mind," she said.

"You're so sweet," he said. His cell phone started ringing, and he hurried off, holding it to his ear.

8. Escape. Burma/Thai border area. September 24, 1988

Maung and Gurney were hiding behind the larger waterfall, below a pool on the face of a low cliff, well enough off the trail to rest and cool their blisters. Maung chewed a piece of bamboo, in a new state, somewhere between waking and sleeping. In this life, daylight, they hid and tried to rest. Nighttime was the only time to dare travel.

Throughout their entire dark journey, across the lush river valley, passing great pagodas, smashed pagodas, burning pagodas drenched in moonlight, stealthily making their way towards Thailand, Maung recited his poetry.

"No beginning, no ending, formless form, inhale, exhale. We do not exist."

Exiles wore paths through the jungle, stumbling past overgrown rice fields, ancient temples, and great reclining Buddhas. Where they were now was very dark wilderness, with much water and many mosquitoes, rolling contours of the place choked with little streams, tree roots, vines, wildlife as if it had a consciousness, as Maung said, "This wants to be a peaceful place." He filled space with his soft voice. "Stroking the earth with our feet, trailing emptiness..."

It was nearly three weeks since they'd left Rangoon. Gurney started having days when she was afraid to speak.

"You don't need to talk," he told her. "But when you're ready, I'm listening."

"I'm okay," she said. It was the second thing she'd said all day.

"I know," he told her. "You're doing great."

"Green, green, green," Maung said. "If it was daylight, everything would be green right now. But at night, it looks so black and white. "He felt her pockets. "You still have your film?"

She was nodding her head.

Maung took Gurney's hand and faced her. "What do you think of this darkness? Photograph this with your imagination. Look. Please," he said. He tickled her in the ribs, kissed her neck. "Don't miss the beauty of this night."

"Thank you," she said. "Thank you." But she was stepping into jungle in the middle of the night, her father dead, her mother missing, and they were stepping into the mud of a massive human exodus.

"See," he looked up at the stars. "The stars are always peaceful. "

Four days earlier, they'd come to Ting Hill and found it burnt to the ground.

"Your Mom is looking up at the stars, just like you are right now. I bet she is," he said. "We'll find her. Don't worry."

Then they came across a huddle of three little children and their big sister who was pregnant, and in labor. There was also an old man, and two middle-aged women. All of them were waiting for the pregnant girl to have her baby. They crouched with banana leaves, held like blankets over the birthing woman. Between the grunts and cries of her labor, they said they hadn't seen any monks or nuns from Ting Hill. They'd seen many professors, many students from the University (the two women and the man were all High School faculty), and promised to keep an ear out for Mya, and pass the word that Gurney would go back to the States via Thailand.

The old man warned them, "Don't pick mangos. They have landmines hanging from all the mango trees near here." The laboring girl cried out, and the women held their hands over her mouth.

It was nearly morning when they found this pool, and Gurney was partly able to clean and pack the hole in Maung's leg, but the small clean hole that had originally been there had changed, become denser, misshapen, filled with pus and blood. It wouldn't quite stop bleeding.

Gurney touched it, gave him a new American words. "Pus."

"Great word," Maung smiled at her, and laughed, honest mirthful laughter. She could tell that he was worried about her. He said, "You and I, no matter what, we share some sort of destiny."

Professor Hyim found Gurney right after he'd found Maung, and he made it his business now to keep them all together. They drove his car as far as they dared, and since then, walked. Maung and Gurney, Professor Hyim, his wife, Aung Soo and her little children: they shared everything. During the day, they hid, and slept. During the night, they traveled. And the closer they came to the border, the greater their sense that their attackers were not finished with them.

Strange shadows covered everything. Gurney didn't trust her eyes. Maung didn't trust his hearing. They held each other by the arms, kissed, touched each other everywhere, lay together in the weeds, kept each other warm.

Professor and Mrs. Hyim worried about Gurney more than about Maung, whose wound wouldn't stop bleeding. The professor practically forced her to chew sugarcane. He told her, "Don't let yourself fall apart, Gurney, you need to keep up your strength. Make the effort to practice mentally healthy thoughts. You'll go back to the states, life will go on.

Ten years from now, you'll be married. You haven't lost your family. You just haven't found it yet."

Gurney said, "Don't say that. I've still got Maung."

Professor Hyim's old eyes crinkled into a question that he directed towards Maung. "Are you going to prepare her?"

"We're fine," she said. They were all looking at her.

"You can't stay," Gurney said.

Professor Hyim took Gurney's hand, waved Maung away. "Let's not talk about that now," he spoke to them all. "Save your energy. Just deal with the present moment, and soon this difficult time will be over."

They passed refugees traveling with rebel troops who gave them more bad news: Tatmadaw had blocked roads to the north and south and was advancing from the West. They had no choice but to keep moving towards Thailand, even in broad daylight.

A moldy potpourri of flowers, leaves, insects, and dirt was crushed together under their feet. During the night, they could sometimes hear children's voices, the squeal of a pig, but now there were more signs of thousands of refugees accumulating along this border.

"I'm staying, you're leaving," he said, and brushed her eyebrows, smiling at her. "And that's that. Forgive me. Your life is in America. Mine is in Burma. Forgive me."

She shook her head. Her feet were covered with holes and hurt. She didn't dare move. It was a swampy place.

"Don't worry." The water came up to their knees. "The crocodiles have all been eaten."

Maung's leg got worse that day after he bumped the bandage. All Gurney's pockets were already torn out. Maung squeezed the hole in his leg shut. "It's not as bad as it looks."

Gurney looked again at Maung's leg, she prodded it gently.

"Look," she said, "The bullet is coming out."

People were excited and relieved as they got closer to the border. "There are trucks on the Thai side," Professor Hyim said. "Must be U.N., or the Red Cross." Professor Hyim kissed his wife. "All we need to do is cross the river."

"I'm going to wait here while you cross," Maung said, and he gestured with his chin.

"Maung," she said.

But he didn't answer her, and she tried to take his hands, but he was stiff.

A bird made a racket in the trees.

"You promised me," she said. "You said you'd marry me."

He cried, kissed her forehead, pressed his lips against her, and said, "Go."

A bird was still warbling, a shrill long note.

"What that?" Gurney asked.

"It's not a bird," he grimaced. "That's your signal! It's time to cross the river!"

Behind them, a band of dust hovered over the horizon. "Thailand is right there, just across the river." He gestured, directed with his hands, finally gave her a strange little shove, "Go!" and then he started to sound angry. "Go, go!"

"I can't," she said. Her legs wobbled. Her feet were swollen, and she tottered as if on high heels.

Maung seemed almost panicky. "Tatmadaw is coming. You need to go without arguing."

"I can't," she said. "I can't leave you too."

Maung took a piece of opium resin from his pocket, pushed it between her lips. "Take some magic carpet," he said. "Fly away, my pretty free bird." And then he picked her up in the air, hoisted her like a sack of rice, both of them shrieking, and threw her over the steep and slippery riverbank, covered in rotten leaves and moss, and she slid down, scraping on her back.

Professor Hyim and the others were at the bottom, and they grabbed her by the arms.

She wailed as they helped her stand back up, "I can't go without Maung!" Professor Hyim's wife shook her to make her stop.

"I hope you don't really believe that," Professor Hyim said, looking her over, chuckling lightly. "He's doing the right thing Gurney. Don't be difficult."

More than a dozen people were already wading in the water. The professor's wife took Gurney's hand. "We will cross the river together," she said, "and all this mud will wash off." They entered the dirty river together under a gray, cloudy sky, and it was cold and stronger than they expected. Gurney had been cold now for days. The currents grew more powerful as they waded deeper. Something exploded above them, not far from the bank.

They were up to their necks in the water.

Professor Hyim said, "Don't worry," but then he slipped in an unexpected hole in the riverbed, and at first he was swimming, but then the current swept him away.

Later, they found Professor Hyim's body on a rock. Thai soldiers came, asked questions. The women and children were escorted to a camp surrounded with barbed wire. In two weeks, the soldiers brought Gurney to an American embassy in Bangkok.

9 A Bridge to Burma: Boston, Massachusetts. November 15, 1999

Gurney dusted off the notebook Maung gave her years ago. Bobby was in school, Robert at work, and the house was quiet. It wasn't that she missed Maung, but that she needed him. Robert couldn't help her with this. She needed Maung.

As far as Borrows knew, Maung never married, and never had children, but had become the self-sacrificing man her mother had warned her about. And Borrows continued to pretend the opium interest was legitimate business. Gurney wondered: would Maung sell opium? Not even if he believed it was legal, if his militia really needed the money, if they could use that money to make an impact?

Borrows' details made Gurney quiver. "God's Army needs food and medicine if nothing else and it's pretty much impossible to sneak through the jungle selling a load of teak. They don't have other moneymaking options. Opium is it."

"So a big company like yours would do business with guerrillas?"

"That's business, Gurney. One day he's a guerrilla, next day, if you're lucky, he's Vice President. Day after that, maybe he's in exile in Switzerland, and that's business. But we aim for smart investments."

"You think Maung is a smart investment?"

Borrows wasn't enjoying this conversation. He didn't want to have to talk about details. "Maung needs every friend he's got. The movement needs every penny it can get, and this could be a big chunk of change. And having Robert inspect the pipeline, what can you possibly say is wrong with that?"

She hung her head, circled Borrows, hands in her pockets, and looked into Bill's eyes. "You're on the pro-democracy side?"

"Of course. For one thing, the good guys speak better English than I do. They go to incredible lengths to educate themselves. They're easier to work with, if you like teak, and I do like teak. I'd like to see that market open up."

"Okay, but why are you involving me? Am I the only Burmese American woman you know?"

"I've been trying to tell you. Maung has been trying to get in touch with you."

"Really."

"Why is that so hard to believe? "

Gurney had to hold one hand on her chest. "Okay," she'd finally said, and cautiously, she shook Borrows' hand. "I am going to believe you."

Gurney put Maung's book away, slid the box back under the bed, yanked sheets, dumped them in the laundry, dragged the vacuum cleaner out. Swirls of curtain were blowing off the window, and the breeze rattled the window frame. Another Boston summer was blowing by.

The vacuum cleaner sucked up a sock. Gurney unclogged it, vacuumed up a spider in the window.

Gurney lay down in bed. Life corrupts people. But Maung would never sell opium. He might give it away, but not sell it.

Gurney felt too anxious to run, so she stretched, counting inhalations and exhalations, imagining a breeze blowing across fields of grass, blowing to the point where she was almost calm. Then her mind filled with distant people that got larger, closer, soldiers in camouflage. Gurney tried to transform them into businessmen in silly ties, but she couldn't get rid of them. She went to make a fresh pot of coffee, with a plan to drink cup after cup of coffee, then run. The phone rang. She picked it up.

"Good morning," Desmond apologized. "I hope you don't mind me calling so early."

"Of course I don't," she said, "I was going to call you later. How goes it?"

"Busy. And I just got something weird in the mail," he said, flustered. "For you."

"Really? Who's it from?"

Desmond said, "It's the weirdest thing, I don't want to tell you too much on the phone. Want to meet me? I'm headed to the Cambridge Café."

"Tell me what it's about."

"I don't want to make it sound like a big deal."

"It already does. Who's it from?"

"I hate to even say this, because you're going to take it wrong."

"Who is it from?"

"I'll tell you when you get here. It was mailed from Bangkok."

Gurney ran, and it was the most effortless run of her life, along the cobbled sidewalk, turning at the light, crossing by the bagel shop, covering the paved part of the trail along the river, passing a woman going the opposite direction, passing homeless and suffering people, passing a bearded, greasy man in a wheelchair pulled by a black lab, passing the old and the poor waiting for the bus at the intersection. Gurney passed a teenage girl in a chilly looking outfit, her blond hair squeaked back into a ponytail, and she ran faster across the strips of green lawn cut between the road and the Charles River. A dry fog was exhausting from the cars, a noxious maritime effect, with noise from the traffic reverberating, amplified under the bridge, where rumpled people were waking up.

Desmond was smearing cream cheese onto a bagel, and he already had his cup of tea. Gurney ordered a coffee, put the sugar to it, and her elated feeling lifted off like a butterfly and was gone. She felt scared. But Desmond was all smiles, and squeezed her shoulder, gesturing towards the door. "Let's sit outside," he said. "It's such a beautiful day."

Gurney knocked the table, sloshed coffee on the sidewalk; Desmond helped her with her chair. He opened his backpack, and took out a creased envelope. They sat on the east side of the shop, soaking in the fragrance of roasting coffee, and the cool morning light.

Gurney tried to make a joke. "No teeth I hope. No wedding band"

Desmond said, "Nothing morbid. Don't worry."

Gurney sighed, sucked on her lower lip, wobbled in her chair.

"He says he found it in her shoe, though," Desmond said, and looked at the table, couldn't meet Gurney's gaze.

"He?" she asked.

"Maung sent it," Desmond blushed. "The letter was addressed to our Grandmother, so I opened it. "

"Maung sent it?" Gurney felt a shadow cross the room, and took a deeper breath, feeling like she might faint.

"He's somewhere in Bangkok, but he doesn't say where exactly. He says your mother is still in Burma, that she is still alive somewhere. Can you believe it? Do you think it could be real?"

Gurney leaned onto the table, dizzy, against his hand. "Cousin," she said, and kissed his hand. "I know," he said, letting her hold his arm where it lay beside the envelope that quivered in the breeze, and they rested, Gurney watching the people on the streets of Harvard Square in her peripheral vision, blurry colors of coats and hats and scarves.

"I am having a good feeling," she said. "I don't want it to go away."

"I know," Desmond told her. "Don't be nervous about it."

Gurney slid the letters out of the envelope. The first was her mother's handwriting, dated a decade earlier. The paper was yellowed, had gotten wet and dried, but still smelled faintly of her mother. "She told me to go back to Boston," Gurney said.

"I know," Desmond said. "I'm glad."

The second page, from Maung was fresh and white, and dated far more recently.

September 9,1999

"Dear Friends,

Sister Rita serves the Ting Hill community, and she brought me the enclosed note, which was signed many years ago by Mya Williams. For a short time I was engaged to be married to Mya's daughter, Gurney Williams, who I last saw under Tatmadaw attack on the Thai/Burma on border in 1988. I want any surviving members of the Wallace and Mya Willams family to know that Mya may still be alive in the jungle near Ting Hill. Myself, I have been a political prisoner for 8 of the past ten years, and have been in the jungle, and am now for a short time in Bangkok. I have not identified Mya in person, but sister Rita says a woman fitting her description gave her this letter, which I enclose to you, which was kept in a shoe. Sister Rita says Mya suffers dementia, or amnesia, and does not remember her own name or how she came to hold the letter. My trusted friend, Maung Ye (card enclosed) is available to help you find Mya, and more. With deepest hope and respect for you in your freedom, and prayers that Mya will be found, and life for all made easier, yours through all times and places, Maung Naing

Gurney held the letters to her face, inhaled. The paper smelled like nothing. Like ink.

Desmond said, "The hair on the back of my neck is lifting straight up!"

"Mommy couldn't possibly still be living in the jungle. "

Desmond said. "Aung Mya was always so strong."

Gurney sat up straight.

"How old would she be now?"

Desmond said, "My mom would be 70 now, and your mom was five years younger."

Gurney shivered, and barely held herself together. "This would be weird, to get my mother back." Her cheeks filled with pressure and tears batted at her lashes. "To introduce her to Bobby." She could get her mother back. That could happen. The sun was shining, but she was blind. Sobbing gleefully into her coffee, she told Desmond about Borrows, and how he must be telling her the truth, and this strange assignment in Burma, Borrows' claim that Maung was looking for her. "Maung is getting ready to do something Desmond. I just don't understand what it is." Desmond absorbed the expression on Gurney's face in his astute brotherly fashion.

"Or, Borrows is just a double duty drug dealer with a fancy schmancy story. If you could confirm what he is saying with Maung, that's one thing. " Desmond said.

"It looks as though this note is saying Maung Ye can find him."

"I wouldn't mention this note to Borrows, Gurney. He might have written it for all you know."

"But this is definitely Maung's handwriting, definitely my mother's writing too," she said, and her voice became melodic and wet. "I'm pretty sure. I mean, who else...."

Desmond said, "If you tell Robert about all this crazy shit, by tomorrow suppertime he'll have your whole family moved across the country, with no forwarding address."

"What do you think I should do?"

"Well," said Desmond, with not a trace of doubt in his trustworthy eyes, "Tell him you've got to go back. Don't make a big deal out of looking for anyone. Keep some of your cards covered. But you've got to go back. You've got to tell him that."

An hour before quitting time, Robert's phone started ringing, and he hoped for Gurney rather than a late-in-the-day client. But it was Bill Borrows.

"We have an important new client, Robert. It's time to let you in on it."

"How important?" A siren screamed outside his window, and Robert couldn't hear half of what Borrows' was saying.

"... worth 2.7 billion, depending on the value of their shares, which will be worth a significant pile of money for us if it all goes through." Borrows spoke as though he'd scalded his throat, or maybe he regretted having to share privileged information with Robert.

"Any percentage of millions and billions sounds good," Robert admitted, but this was the kind of conversation that went over his head. He preferred it when Borrows spoke more directly. "What's this about?"

"A competitor of my former employer, Merger Petroleum and Gas," Borrows cleared his throat. He said, "Merger, and others, a consortium of interested partners, including fuel industries from Canada and France, and the business branch of the Government of Myanmar, will all be working together as a team. It's, you know, a big deal. Even bigger than a couple of billion, the whole project will be like 18 billion. So, I'm not buffing my nails here, but you can thank me."

Robert eased into his desk chair, switching the phone to his other ear, rubbing the one he'd crushed with the receiver. "Thank you," he said, but he wasn't sure he understood correctly. "Is this like, an investment?"

"No, Robert, my son, it's an adventure!" Borrows' voice had a funny edge to it. Robert didn't want to risk his job, but working with China was hard enough. Robert pressed on his twitching eyebrow. "We're in a consortium with…a dictatorship?" he asked. Maybe it was a joke.

"I don't think you'll be meeting with any dictators, Robert. Sure, the Burmese have a long history of class-ism, slavery, that sort of thing. I don't intend to put my cultural mores onto them, but yes, you'll have to keep your eyes really open."

"Burma Myanmar has one of the most repressive military dictatorships on the face of the planet." Robert took a breath. Counted to himself. "Keep my eyes open? I'm not going to work over there."

"C'mon Robert, this will be fun as hell. Don't you remember that character in the Chairman Mao jacket? What was his name? Cheng? Remember how he was with the yoga balls? That turned out pretty well, eh?"

Robert looked up. His office door was swinging open. It startled him.

"Someone's here."

"I know. I sent her over. Julia seemed to think she could talk you into this. She brought you a contract you need to sign, a little waiver, not a big deal. This is all last minute, sorry. My personality and your personality, I know sometimes we clash, but Rob, trust me. You need to go with this. I really mean that. I'm not going to take no for an answer."

"Is this going to be anything like that big learning experience you had over there when ARCO pulled out, when you said, never again?"

"Negotiations West-East can be tricky, no doubt about it, a fair amount of politics involved. That's why I need you. That's what I'm thinking. You know these armchair bureaucrats."

"Tell me all about it."

"They don't go anywhere until all the research is done and the ducks lined up. We'll be working as their representatives. We're doing inspections. If the biggies like our report, they come out and pass papers. The seal of royalty. It's all ritual and posturing, and I will guide you every step of the way. This is an extremely lucrative transaction, Robert."

"I don't doubt it, Bill."

"If inspections are what matter to you, Robert, I'm telling you, you should do it."

When Robert got home that night, Gurney was in a fabulous mood and she already knew. Julia had called her too, given her the gist of it, and Robert thought, we can't be talking about this. We can't even be thinking about it.

"I don't know," he said, shaking his head. "I strongly suspect an ulterior motive."

She agreed from across the room, where she was brushing her teeth at the bathroom door. She rinsed and spit, brought him a glass of water.

"You have a connection with Borrows," Robert said. "Maybe you're a better judge of his character than I can be."

"Are you kidding Robert? I know nothing about your boss. Absolutely nothing."

"I'm depending on you to be straight with me," he told her. "If there's anything I should know, tell me. I just don't want to get into a dangerous situation. Bottom line."

Gurney said, "I can't help you avoid danger. It's dangerous just being alive."

"It didn't sound too strenuous, though, from an actual working perspective," Robert replied. "No shovels involved, not even many notes. Just a tour of the border, visit to a pipeline, photos."

"With a military escort?"

"Hopefully not," he told her. "Bill says we could have at least a few afternoons when nobody's watching us. He says the military gives couples more opportunities than singles to roam around unsupervised. So Bill is bringing Julia too. He's calling it a working vacation."

Gurney's dimples were appearing and reappearing, and Robert loved her dimples. "Ha, ha" she said. He laughed. "Ha, ha."

Robert fell into his chair, and Gurney was dancing around in her pink flannel nightgown, her eyebrows up, and hair bobbing. For ten years he'd told her, forget it, let Burma go, she was never going to find her parents' bodies, she was never going to find out what happened to Maung, she was never going to go back there. Never.

He said, "This might be disappointing for you. Anti-climatic. We'll just go and look around and leave."

"Probably." Gurney picked out a map from her bookcase, unfolded it on the bed. With two fingers she traced areas along a coast, up to the border between Myanmar and Thailand. "It was a very pretty area of the world," Gurney said. "Slave labor is most intense all along this border. The whole area has been denuded by the constant influx of refugees."

"Have you got this straight?" Robert asked. "This trip could possibly lead to a deal between Merger Gas and the Myanmar military? "

"Of course not," she said. "You don't have to sign any deals, Robert. I think we are supposed to pretend. Give them the run-around. Drive them insane with paperwork."

"Gurney, these people are the experts in torture, not me! And I don't want to piss them off," he answered.

"I would LOVE to piss them off Robert."

"We have our own son to think about."

"Robert. I have my whole family to think about."

A moldy coffee cup was on the bedside table, and Robert picked it up, set it back down.

She said, "Borrows is going to send someone over there. Why can't it be us? It's fate. We go, and give the dictatorship a small headache."

"Journalists are locked out." Robert said. "You can't go as a photographer."

"We'll be undercover as "businessmen.""

"I really am a business man."

"That's what makes you so perfect for this. You do your job, and I'll do mine."

Robert looked at her. She was very pretty.

He said. "Your excitement is somewhat contagious."

"We could do anything," she told him. "We could drive out to the country, sneak around a little, visit a labor camp, a prison camp. Refugee camps. Who knows what we'll find?"

He clapped his knees in mock enthusiasm and went through a mental checklist, trying to enumerate everything that made this idea officially as crazy and impossible as it sounded. "We could find slave labor and border bombings. That would be great. I'm really cut out for that. This is exactly why I didn't sign up for the army."

"I didn't expect this would be so scary for you," she said. "I'm not scared."

"I'd have to be totally honest about whatever I saw," he warned her. "And I'm not sure that your opinion of the Myanmar military, or even of Merger Gas is as objective as mine will need to be. What if I decide to give them the go ahead with their plans? Energy is energy. Every nation needs energy. That's the only aspect of this thing that I know anything about."

"I'd expect nothing less of you, Robert. I would never want you to do anything you didn't believe in."

They had a late dinner. Bobby was asleep when they were finally getting into bed.

Robert asked, "What if they cart you off to prison from the airport?"

"Why on earth would anyone do that?" she asked. She pulled an old cotton nightgown on over her head, and he pulled it back off.

"Because you're on somebody's list of subversives?" He meant it as a joke.

She wrapped her arms around him, planting a serious kiss on his lips.

"Record keeping sucks in third world countries. Besides, Myanmar is into tourism these days. It would be a terrible blow to both tourism and exports if the Myanmar military hauled the wife of a Merger Gas inspector off to jail." She said, "I think this will be good for us." She was naked, and her face was soft and happy. Robert nearly fell over in love, watching her.

"I don't trust Bill all that much," Robert said. Bill was a good guy to work for in many ways, but not because he was scrupulous. Gurney rubbed her body against him.

"Don't be paranoid," she said, and then she slid into bed, holding open the covers for him.

Robert got into bed. The whole day had been exhausting and perplexing, but also, he was surprised to find this idea excited him, too. He was fifty years old. What had he done with his life? What had he really done with his wife? Maybe they needed an adventure.

119

"We couldn't make the situation in Burma any worse," Gurney said.

And she was right. It was an opportunity, fallen into his lap, and who else, given his history, his resume, his wife, could possibly be better suited to investigate working conditions along the border of Myanmar?

Robert thought of something. "This wasn't your idea to get me this job, right?"

Covers falling around her waist, an exasperated expression on her face, she said, "Of course not."

"Say it," he said. His worries had already spoiled her dimples; might as well get it all out in the open.

She hesitated. "I'm thinking about my mother, and father, and Maung, and what they'd say. Robert, they'd want us to go. They would have loved you so much Robert."

"They wouldn't have had a chance to meet me. You would have been married to someone else."

"You kind of remind me of my Dad."

He said, "And we didn't even need a therapist to find it out."

"I never thought of it before. But you do, actually."

Robert laid his head on her chest, listened to her heart.

Everything about her felt right: the dangerous parts, the safe parts, and the way she pushed him into this foreign territory, all the ways she was a challenge. He steeled himself. Gurney wanted to go. He'd never been good at making her happy.

"You know that story," she said, "About how when you love something, you have to let it go?"

He shifted in the bed, touched her face, and held his face close to hers. "No," he said.

10. Freedom by Maung Naing

Power is not freedom, not without the Soul.

The Free Buddha, Jesus, Mahatma Ghandi, Aung San Suu Kyi, does not make this choice.

The soul makes this choice.

To kill or not kill.

You still have your power when you kill my mother,

when you take away my baby

and burn her alive.

But listen to me,

you have no freedom, sucking blood

off the mosquito bitten backs

of babies making brick in mud holes.

Your punctured hollow soul

has deflated at the end of poles prodding elephants

chained to your teak.

Free Buddhist, Free Christian, Free Muslim that you think you are,

reciting profanity, you kill your soul,

you kill, denying that you kill,

killing your own freedom

your secrets cleaving you from a hungry soul,
burying all your treasure with the dead.

11. God's Army. Oct. 18, 1999, Bangkok.

Maung shared his mattress with Moe and two others.
It wasn't uncomfortable, Maung appreciated the bed, but it
was crowded in this particular corner of a monstrous sprawl
of shacks in the San Pulau neighborhood of Bangkok, a
neighborhood made of corrugated metal, scrap wood, torn
sheets of fabric, cardboard and plastic, a car hood between
stacked cinder blocks, broken wooden pallets and wire, on a
precious slab of concrete, and thousands of refugees, fleeing
Tatmadaw attacks. They hid with other impoverished people
in plain sight, each shack knitted into the others, sharing the
most practical advantages of a post or bag of cement, and
spigot. You always had to wait in line for water. The sewer
troughs were always full. But you could sleep on a mattress,
under a roof, and that felt good.

Tatmadaw sometimes crossed border areas into
Thailand and sometimes lobbed bombs into Thailand, but
Bangkok was far enough away from the border that you only
had to worry about Thai government and police as you
regrouped, collected supplies, and prepared to face the jungle
again. Sometimes a social worker came through to look at the
babies. But Thai Police never came into the slum, not even to
put out a fire, not even if you begged them. Rats would run
across you, even chew on you while you were trying to sleep;

but if the social workers came, they'd bring medicine, and the mosquitoes were worse in the jungle. So, when Sister Rita heard Maung was out of prison and in Bangkok, she was sure she'd find him here. She gave him Mya's letter.

Until that moment, Maung thought both Gurney and Mya had died. Otherwise, they would have found him in prison, they would have sent him food, contacted him. Sister Rita told Maung that the woman she believed was Mya was living with other survivors of the Ting Hill Monastery massacre. She told him, when war separates you, everything goes wrong all at once. Gurney might have been looking for him, but she could never have found him. And Mya didn't remember anything from before the massacre. Rita told Maung, "Sometimes you make me think of a spoiled little boy. They didn't abandon you. They lost you, just as you lost them. "

It took Maung a week, but he posted Mya's letter back to the states. It was of course an impossible dream, every aspect of it, like flinging a wish to the stars. But still, they were like family to him. He had been so in love with her. His own parents and siblings now were all missing or dead. If it was possible they were still alive, if doing this could help Gurney find with her mother, he wanted to help. And he needed help too. If anyone was still alive who could help him, he thought, it might be someone in Gurney's family.

The pants Moe was wearing were too large and falling off.

Maung said. "Thank you, Moe, for the rice, and the roof. "

Skinny Moe re-adjusted his rope belt, tied it up high around his waist. He said, "And I thank you." They climbed out onto a wobbly corrugated roof. From there, sticks led down to a pallet gate that spilled on twisted wire hinges into a wet alleyway.

An old widow who sold garlic at the market was their landlord, but charged them nothing but to peel garlic. Now she was in the alley scrubbing clothes in a bucket of soapy water. Maung and Moe peeled garlic while she did laundry, and when she left, they had the rest of the boring day to themselves.

Sometimes Red Dog stuck around with them all day, and all he wanted to do was gamble and talk about someday making money, having a family, getting a bike. They also talked about poetry, spiritual beliefs, philosophy and politics, but only when they drank. Then they discussed what it means to be human, and why humans kill humans.

It passes time, Maung thought, but it's not productive. Any day, Thai police would find them, send them back to the border where Myanmar would throw them in jail again. If they were going to get arrested anyway, Maung wanted to be arrested doing something worthwhile. They talked about actions they could take from inside Thailand.

"Commander Kyaw says the Righteous Warriors of Burma are harvesting teak, exporting it black-market through Singapore," Moe said. "They need more soldiers, Maung."

"I bet."

"They're counting a whole city of people now, 20,000 people out there in the jungle," Moe said, "and they're pretty beaten up."

Red Dog shuffled a deck of cards. His arms were beefy compared to Moe's. He said, "People need rice, medicine. There is nothing political about that. It's a real job Maung."

"Unless the Righteous Warriors pay off Tatmadaw as well as you, it's a dead man's job. "

Moe's face wrinkled. He said, "Maung, I ask you seriously, who else is there besides us to fight back?"

"Harvesting teak isn't fighting back."

"There are other jobs." Moe tapped on his forehead. "Commander Kyaw had a special idea for famous intellectuals like you."

"What's that?"

"Take over the Myanmar Embassy in Thailand." Moe tossed Maung a floor plan. "Hold a press conference to draw international attention to Myanmar's attacks."

Maung grinned. "Ha ha," he said, "Ha ha ha. Very funny."

Moe complained, "It's not funny. It's serious. Think about the embassy. There are phones, computers, soda machines. Everything. And everybody loves you. Thai police won't dare shoot you."

Maung said, "Thai police won't have any idea who Maung Naing is."

"You're too humble Maung! You have friends all over the world. Now's the time! We can save lives, Maung."

Maung couldn't answer. It broke his heart to see Moe so hopeful.

Red Dog shrugged, took out a cigarette. "Life is fucking ridiculous."

Moe said, "Maung. You can translate too. This is exactly what poets are supposed to do. Communicate. Let the world know our situation."

"But I don't know how to express our situation," Maung said, aghast to think he once thought like a poet.

"I could help you write it," Moe said and Red Dog shoved him. "But I have writer's block."

A stream of rusty water ran down the edge of the window, puddling at their feet.

Red Dog said, "Ne Win and his comrades aren't guilty of ethnic cleansing until Time Newsweek says they are."

Red Dog showed off weapons Commander Kyaw had supplied.

Maung swatted a mosquito. "The headlines will read: former poet activist blows up tripping over his own hand grenade." But after hours of talking about it, they worked out a plan; and they put it into play soon after.

They entered the Myanmar Embassy in Bangkok in the middle of the day.

Workers ordinarily eat lunch at 11 a.m., so they'd decided on 11:15, when the embassy would be mostly empty. Moe and Red Dog pulled masks over their faces. Moe held out a grenade, shouted, "drop to the floor or die!" And everyone dropped.

Tribe educated, university educated, refugee camp educated, it was some kind of strange new talent that now allowed Maung to stand in the embassy doorway as though he owned it. The street surged with activity and soon it was full of uniforms: Thai police, Thai military, Security.

When Maung lived at the camp, he couldn't do anything but sleep. Now, he began to feel something. You find yourself carrying old people and babies, pulling children by the arms, dragging a cooking pot and old family photographs, feet bloody and swollen, with an empty belly and a dry mouth, and you must bury the dead.

What is a poet supposed to do in a situation like this?

But maybe, if something were to change, he wouldn't need to be a soldier anymore. He could become a poet again.

Sometimes we have to endure foul tastes, biting insects, diarrhea, exhaustion, and hunger. A person can endure and survive. In Insein Prison they forced him to stand in a bucket of water, night and day. He wasn't a troublemaker before, not even as a kid. Never played with guns, not toy guns even. At four or five years old, he put his hand up to the window screen at bedtime to feed the mosquitoes. When he was a child, he couldn't kill a fly. But after thirteen nights, on the fourteenth day even the electric prod couldn't make him stand, but Maung stood now. He held a grenade against his belly.

Hostages were crying, and another thing—his leg was bothering him. Vessels died in there. Nerves were exposed. Invisible parts of him had permanent damage. He had to learn to live with pain.

After the first few hours in the embassy, he tried to think through his situation in an organized way.

None of this was the fault or responsibility of any one person. He didn't quite know how it happened, or how he came to be there. One person can't start a war. But one person is responsible for small things, for letting small things happen. Each day educated people, neat as a pin, careful people, get up and turn their backs as others are killed, tortured.

If Gurney was still alive, she was American now.

Maung never expected to live even this long. But maybe, if she was alive in the United States, she could help. She could take pictures, write a story. But the police controlled the phone lines at the embassy, and there had been no reporters, no interviews.

His leg twitched, forcing him to shift his weight, and compare what happened to his leg to what Tatmadaw did to Win Low.

Win Low was torn open, left sprawled in the garden all night long, crying. Win Low's family could only peer from their hut, listen to him cry until he was dead. Even then, after his body stiffened in rigor mortis, and softened again, even after it began to bloat and smell in the rain, the soldiers wouldn't let Win Low's family collect the body. The soldiers made a bonfire, roasted a pig. They stayed four days.

If he got the chance, he'd tell the media about Win Low. Gurney could visit him, bring him food the next time he went to prison. He should have married her, she would have found him, visited him. After all those years in prison, maybe she was alive somewhere.

Maung looked out a window, lit a cigarette. Someone whispered. A woman in the room began whimpering. Today, whimpering over nothing annoyed him. He had a short temper. In the big scheme of things, if that woman could do nothing else with her life, right now she didn't need to cry. No one ought to cry. Crying is useless.

Maung held up his grenade silently over his head, scanned the courtyard through the window, and looked around the room, to decide who was crying. But the room was quiet again.

Tatmadaw gave his parents ten minutes to leave, and burnt their house to the ground.

Maung moved his weight to rest entirely on his good leg.

Commander Kyaw told them this: sometimes you have to fight fire with fire.

Thirty-eight hostages were sitting on the floor of the embassy conference room. Maung's job involved watching them, and also watching out the window. The hostages were not resisting and were not difficult to watch.

Moe wants you on the phone now, Maung," Red Dog waved Maung over, and added in a loud voice, "We are fighting for peace and justice. Are you fighting for peace and justice?"

But the hostages didn't understand his language.

One of the hostages—a businessman in western dress, a gem trader—wiped his face with his jeweled hand. The woman sitting next to him had dark streaks on her cheeks from her tears and mascara. Maung took Red Dog's cigarette out of his mouth. "Don't smoke around grenades," Maung said.

Red Dog laughed at Maung's relief as he put it out. "A cigarette won't make it explode."

"How do you know that?" Maung asked.

Moe gestured for Maung to take back the grenade, "Here, I'll show you," but Maung shook his head, backed away. "Don't fuck around," he said.

Another truck rumbled to a stop in the courtyard.

Moe said, "English language newspaper on the phone."

Maung spoke into a receiver, but the connection wasn't good and hadn't spoken English for a long time. Maung struggled to understand. The accent was American. A woman. At first, he thought he might be talking to Gurney.

A tattered Myanmar flag was draped against a wall behind him; Red Dog had ripped it into strips. Maung traced a jade medallion decorating the teakwood embassy desk, manufactured under military supervision, and held the phone to his ear.

"Can you confirm for me how many hostages you have?" the woman asked.

Maung talked to her. Their plan was working! He thought, everything will change! Look at South Africa! "I write for the Bangkok Post," the woman said.

"Good, good!" Maung said, but his stomach was upset. It wasn't an American paper.

"How many hostages did you say?"

The hand holding the receiver was shaking. His arms were tired. He wanted to talk about Win Low, but instead said, "We have thirty-eight hostages."

"Tell her our demands!" Moe insisted.

Maung said, "We say to Myanmar, release all political prisoners, enter into talks with elected President Aung San Suu Kyi. We ask the world to put pressure on Myanmar."

Maung couldn't understand what the reporter was saying now.

The connection got worse. "Hello? Hello?" He hung up the phone. The line was dead. Red Dog put a grenade back in Maung's hands.

When he was younger, he never believed in God or the devil though his mother was a good Christian, and his father was a good Buddhist, and Maung felt free to believe whatever he wanted to believe. But now, he changed his thinking. Now, he believed in the devil in the Tatmadaw soldiers, who took Tun Tun and Saw Tin Oo from a meal of rice, pulled them outside, made them kneel, and shot them in the head in front of their children; and in Tatmadaw who took farmers, children, old people, forced them to dig ditches during rice-planting season, twelve feet wide, 8 feet deep, thirty-three miles through the jungle, and the rice wasn't planted.

Maung leaned against a window ledge. Tried to remember what it felt like to be free, to have a soul. He justified the state of his mind.

Aung San Suu Kyi is famous, but even she cannot change the world. If she is free, it is not the sort of freedom that allows her to leave her yard. She can't stop Tatmadaw from ransacking, from killing. Aung San Suu Kyi, free martyr of Burma; and Tatmadaw, the devil. They were like two arms

135

of the same beast. What does it take for one arm to protect the other?

His parents were murdered. Gurney's father was murdered. Maybe Gurney was destroyed too. So many friends, parents, neighbors, professors were murdered. He felt sick of it, sick of having no freedom, sick of no choice but to be doing this.

The businessman in the suit stood up.

"I only want to stretch my legs," he said, in Thai language.

Maung said, "Okay." It was uncomfortable, holding this grenade, and Maung wondered when he could set it down again.

On the trail over Pat Tan Pass, with Tatmadaw following behind, then he'd longed for a live grenade. But now, grenades were nerve-wracking and unpleasant to hold.

Next morning, still in the Embassy, Maung leaned against the teak desk, and spoke on the phone again, reading two demands:

"We demand the Myanmar Military State Law and Order Restoration Council, previously known as the State Peace and Development Council, immediately free all political prisoners."

"Yes," the reporter said. The phone line was good. The Thai government had stepped out of the way.

"And we demand the Myanmar military immediately enter into talks with National League for Democracy leader Aung San Suu Kyi," Maung said.

"But Aung San Suu Kyi is opposed to your action," the reporter said. "I was allowed to speak with her today. She is dismayed by what you are doing. This is the first act of violence by Burmese nationals in exile in Thailand."

Maung commanded himself to be calm, wanted to tell about Win Low, but he hung up the phone.

"What did they say?" Moe asked. Paw Law was there too. He stood by the door, looking out into the courtyard, and a street-side door, and a row of windows at Thai police, Thai military, and Thai soldiers. And themselves, they were only four armed men!

"The media is saying we are a band of violent radicals," Maung said.

They all laughed nervously. Red Dog used to be a pharmacist. Moe had studied botany. Paw Law was a schoolteacher.

One of Moe's cigarettes smoldered on the floor, and Maung ground it out with his sandal. They were hot and sweaty. The hostages passed around a box of cookies.

Moe said, "Maybe someday we'll get a Christian leader, instead of a Buddhist, and things will be different."

"Yes. Things would be different. The Pope would visit," Maung said.

They laughed.

Moe lit up a new cigarette, and looked out the window.

The street was closed, cluttered with military trucks and police cars.

Outside, car doors were slamming in the courtyard. If the Thai military wanted to kill them, they were already dead.

Maung felt his knees quivering, but he said, "We must be very careful not to discharge our weapons, in honor of Aung San Suu Kyi, even if we are attacked."

Moe retorted, "Christians allow for fighting fire with fire."

"Not Martin Luther King," Maung said. "Or your hero, Nelson Mandela. He was a Christian. True Christians are non-violent."

"What was Malcolm X?" Red Dog asked.

"Existentialist."

"No, he was Muslim."

"Stop discussing it," Paw Law retorted. A vehicle roared by with the horn blasting. "All religions are violent."

"My religion is non-violent," Maung said.

"Then what are you doing here?" Red Dog said. "Don't be a hypocrite when you are fighting a war."

"I've eaten the body of Christ, and it made me a different man! " Moe exclaimed, "When we are done with this, Moe, you should eat the body of Christ! It gives you strength! Doesn't it, Maung?"

Maung said, "I could use some body-of-Christ right now."

"But be careful what you say," Moe answered. "It's bad luck."

Then hostages needed water, and to go to the bathroom, and to make phone calls. Moe made more phone calls. Maung told a reporter, "We are only a botanist, a pharmacist, a school teacher and a poet." They waited.

"Maybe Johnny Htoo will become President of Burma," Moe was saying.

"Let's hope not!" Maung replied, but Moe was only joking. Johnny and Luther Htoo were child-soldiers leading God's Army; less than 12 years old, having survived several attacks, they were supposed to have supernatural powers.

Maung was exhausted. Maybe a government of little children is just what the world needs. From moment to moment, nothing and everything seemed possible. Maung noticed the woman, eyes swollen from crying, holding a string

139

of Buddhist prayer beads. He felt bad about her. He wanted to let her go home.

It was six o'clock. They let the women hostages and the old man go home.

"We're in over our heads," Maung said.

"God's on our side," said Moe, but Maung couldn't tell if he was joking or serious.

At 8 o'clock that evening Moe said, "I heard my name on the radio. Now I'm famous too."

The rest of the hostages left at 9. The Righteous Burmese Warriors negotiated their own surrender and release with a Thai military man, and they were all escorted by helicopter back to the Myanmar border.

"Don't come back into Thailand again," the pilot told them. "Next time, we might have to kill you. Even your poet." He told Maung, "I don't even like your poetry."

12. Co-Parenting

Boston, Massachusetts. January 14, 2000

Desmond was worried about Bobby. Gurney had kept too many secrets, and Robert was permissive to the point of negligence. It seemed like Bobby might have secrets too. He was sulky one moment, and innocent the next. Eleven years old is a weird age. He was right on the cusp of it, where it seemed he was either going to turn out to be a great kid, or he was going to start smoking cigarettes and playing with knives and guns. It was freezing cold. January sucks. With Gurney and Robert in Burma, tending their home fires wasn't a bad trade for his boring day-to-day single life. Desmond was prepared for a little bit of drama. He expected Bobby to test him.

Best thing to do in an afternoon in January is curl up with a book, but Bobby wasn't home from after-school yet, and he should be. Desmond thought, I'd never make a good househusband, but being a househusband was all he ever wanted to be. He shoveled their walk, made lentil soup, and unloaded the dishwasher. It was not quite five p.m., but already dark out.

Desmond had invited Bobby and a few of his friends to go after-school bowling, but Bobby and his friends didn't like bowling.

"What do you like?" Desmond asked. It was kind of insulting, Bobby's attitude. Desmond wasn't used to his teenager guise. The ten-year old Bobby had seemed a lot sweeter. "Ever since that whole fireworks thing, you've been incredibly unfriendly."

Bobby retorted, "The fireworks have nothing to do with anything."

The phone rang. It was Bobby.

"Desmond, can you come pick me up?"

"Don't you want to walk?"

Bobby was silent. Desmond heard the wind howl and felt like a stupid ass.

"It's minus 10 degrees," Bobby said.

Desmond said, "I'm just trying to remember where the keys are."

"On the key-hook. By the door."

"Got it," Desmond said. "Give me ten minutes."

"Thanks, Desmond," Bobby said, and for the first time since his parents left, Bobby sounded almost friendly.

Desmond put on his outside gear, opened the front door, and snow kicked up into his face. His ears froze almost immediately, and he wished he had a scarf. His eyes watered and his lashes began to freeze together. The car door was frozen shut. Desmond went back to the house for a box of matches, tried thawing the lock by heating the key.

A neighbor came out, and banged and thumped on her car door, cracked it open, started it, leaving a plume of exhaust pouring out, closer and closer to Desmond, who couldn't unlock the car. Finally he went inside, waited for the teakettle, and poured hot water over the door. That did the trick. His mittens made it difficult to turn the key, and his bare hands hurt in the cold, but he pumped on the pedals, and the car was a good one, it started right up.

Sometimes house-sitting left Desmond feeling a little bit emotional. Being a father figure, even temporarily, is a big responsibility. He spent several minutes trying to adjust the seat, mirrors, and wheel. He talked out-loud to himself, practicing saying things to Bobby. "I'm sorry if I screw up and am boring," he said to the mirror. He tried a quirky grin and said, "When you're my age, you'll be boring too."

Being a social activist is a bit deviant, when you think about it. Robert looks down on him. What kind of nitwit collects $45,000 in college debt, gets a double Ph.D., and has nothing better to do in January than housesit? Robert probably earns $120,000 a year? $150,000? And has a liberal arts degree! Desmond got $25,000 a year and a cheap deal on rent. He didn't even have health insurance. But as long as the Massachusetts Burma law goes through, he thought, I'll be happy. Someone had to devote some time to this stuff. Passing laws costs money and time. Desmond needed a job that didn't cost him so much of both.

Gurney had Buddhist prayer beads hanging from the Volvo's mirror. He couldn't remember if he'd turned down the lentil soup.

The school turn-around was covered with ice and sand. A handful of kids came running into the cold and dark. One kid pulled his mittens off, lit a cigarette under the streetlight. Desmond parked and tried to get out of the car, but his door was frozen shut again. Bobby came running up, sweatshirt pulled up half over his head, coat flapping in the wind, covered with snow, heaving along a backpack that looked at least a third his size. He slammed the backpack into the passenger door, and cracked it open.

"Mom called me at school today," Bobby said, sounding peeved, tired. The driving was slippery, awful. "I can't believe she called me at school."

"In Burma, it's four o'clock in the morning right now. They're sleeping. When did you expect her to call? "

Bobby said, "I don't like it when you talk to me that way."

"What way?"

Bobby was quiet.

"Bobby, what's wrong with you lately?"

Desmond heard something that sounded like a sob. "She's still in love with Maung," Bobby said.

It was the last thing in the world he expected to hear. Desmond rested longer than he really needed to at the stop sign.

"She didn't say that."

"No, I just know that." Bobby had pulled a tissue out of his book-bag, blew his nose. "That was a long wait. My mother doesn't usually leave me waiting that long."

"I'm so sorry Bobby," Desmond said.

"I don't think this whole thing is safe. If it was safe, she would have brought me."

"They won't get into trouble," Desmond said. And took a breath. "And she said if she found him, she'd take his picture."

"I know," Bobby said. "I hope she does."

They pulled into the driveway and went into the house, which smelled like burnt lentil soup. They ordered a pizza, which was a better idea anyway. Bobby stretched cheese and asked Desmond, "How can you be sure which are the good guys and which are the bad guys? Do they have different uniforms?"

"Sometimes it's hard to tell," Desmond said, and he made a joke that he later apologized for. "I just keep an eye on the ones with the most money," Desmond joked. "They are the bad guys."

13. The Poet Soldier

By Maung Naing

A twin man,

One hand stops the killing,

The other carries the gun.

I have already been killed, so I'm not afraid to

Curl myself in your barbed wire,

To answer your

Questions, to use

One hand to feed you, and one to drop bombs on your

head.

The soul that was, is dead.

It held a loaded gun to its own head.

14. Boy Soldiers

October 20, 1999

Burma loomed below them like a big green animal, lumpy and disheveled, blue-brown rivers leaking through folds in the skin. The helicopter descended and put them out, wind whipping, stumbling under the weight of their own thin bodies, and they all fell to the ground as though prostrating themselves. The Thai machine flew off, and they were in a clearing on the side of a small mountain. Then Moe yelled after the helicopter, whooped, threw his shirt off, and spun it over his head. They'd worried the whole trip that Tatmadaw would kill them as soon as the helicopter landed, but the mountain was quiet. They were still alive.

It as one of the happiest moments of his life, Moe cheering like that, safely walking that steep and muddy road. They traveled across a narrow bridge to a camp on a ragged corner of Thailand, Maung's bad leg wobbling with fatigue. A God's Army guard met them, and brought them to a hut. In the morning, Mr. David woke them up, saying, "No duck, no pork, no eggs, no swearing, no womanizing."

At breakfast, Maung saw the twin colonels. They were wrapped in each other's arms, holding a blanket, their eyes the biggest things on their faces, foreheads casting shadows over sunken hungry cheeks. "You are famous," they said. The occupation of the Myanmar Embassy had been non-stop on the radio. God's Army had been struggling to get public attention in Thailand. "We have 20,000 refugees. We need the wealthy Thais to donate money if we hope to keep our people from starving to death, or dying of malaria."

Settled onto banana leaf mats, strategizing, the twins had a can of water simmering on a dry twig and grass fire, and they held their hands over the fire. The guard kept it blazing, avoiding smoke.

The boys both bent their elbows in a childish way, pushed hair off their faces.

"Did Mr. David tell you the rules?" Luther asked. His voice was raspy.

"Yes," They answered. Luther's arms weren't even as thick as a piece of sugar cane. Maung checked his own arm. Luther lit a cheroot and smoked. Luther said, "Can one of you can read scriptures to me?"

Maung said, "I'll read."

"Read to me from the book of Corinthians, then," Luther said.

The pages were marked with string. Maung read aloud, "But God hath chosen the foolish things of the world to

149

confound the wise; and God hath chosen the weak things of the world to confound the things which are mighty."

"Now from the book of Timothy," Luther said, and Maung found another spot in the bible. "Fight the good fight, lay hold on eternal life, where unto thou art also called."

Reading poetry can be like eating a good meal, and Maung nearly cried with relief and happiness. "Out of the shadow of the devil, into the light of the divine," he said.

"You sense the existence of the God of the Holy Mountain," Luther told him.

The Burmese Righteous Warriors agreed to help God's Army.

In early January, Tatmadaw set up a camp directly across the river, so God's Army stayed in Thailand, and through binoculars, watched Tatmadaw soldiers setting up mortars. There was real work to do, mystical order in the heart of chaos. Tatmadaw could see them, but not fire on them.

Karen tribal people flowed like a river out of the hills, carrying babies, old people, corpses, wounded, exhausted, pooling all along the border. On two-way radio, Maung listened to God's Army advising refugees to avoid traveling further north, but to cross the river as soon as possible. Maung climbed a tree. He could see the Thai/Burma gas pipeline, a ragged gash with smoke hanging over it cut from the bottom of the jungle, stretching like a highway towards the Bay of Bengal.

Maung said, "It's not owned by Thailand, and not by Tatmadaw either. It is like a separate world, with a government of it's own."

Luther and Johnny nodded heads and smoked. Luther climbed up past Maung's shoulders, and looked through a binocular. His feet were thick with dirty callus. He said, "We should try to trade with them."

"Go invite them to trade with us," Johnny said. And the twins began taking turns, with the other camp children, sliding down a loamy bank on the broken cardboard noodle box. God's Army, with RBW, packed up camp, and wrapped the radio up.

Thai aircraft started buzzing overhead at dawn.

God's Army and Righteous Burmese Warriors split into four groups of eight soldiers each. Maung's patrol helped refugees wading across the river, crossing brazenly back and forth near the bridge, to the edge of the Burmese jungle, and back across the river. Maung helped a woman, her old mother, and a ten-year-old boy (an orphan).

Maung pulled maggots from a wound in an old woman's foot. "He had two little sisters, 2 and 3 years old," the old woman said. The boy didn't cry as she explained, "The soldiers shot his father and threw his sisters in the fire."

Suddenly, a low aircraft approached. Then the sound of the propeller was drowned in a tremendous explosion. "They just blew up the bridge!" Red Dog said.

People were dropping everything. Another explosion. They all began to run. The helicopter had swerved south and come back to hover over the river. An old man stepped off the trail, a basket sparkled sunlight just long enough to reflect excitement in the man's face. An explosion knocked Maung to the ground.

They found a small cave, a pocket of dirt near the top of the bank and rolled under it. They saw a mortar in the air, dragging its tail across the river from the Thai side. Still, Maung couldn't understand it.

"Did Tatmadaw enter Thailand?"

Red Dog pointed, "That's not Tatmadaw! That is the Thai army! They won't let us enter Thailand."

"No," Maung said.

He couldn't believe it. Below in the river, a woman was wading in the water, holding a wrapped bundle in her arms. He saw her staggering towards Thailand, the bundle struggling in her upraised arms, chest deep in the water.

Maung fell down the embankment, and entered the river, his weapon dragged in the water.

Merger Gas supports the Universal Declaration of Human Rights. The challenge is how to translate these principles into practice." Human Rights and Merger Gas: A Discussion Paper

15. On the Plane   January 10, 1999

On the plane, Gurney and Robert sat across the aisle from a Chinese-American whose name was "Ivan Sullivan. Junior. My father was Scottish/English, and my mother Chinese-American. Gurney's an interesting name. Where'd that one come from?"

"Her mother was an ambulance driver," Robert said.

Gurney turned to Ivan. "I'm named after a bird, Gurney's Pitta. It was supposed to be extinct, but they found some still living in Burma."

Bill turned around in his seat to talk to her. "I didn't know that. You're named after a rare bird? That makes sense. And, Gurney," his voice lowered, "if you don't mind, don't call it Burma while we're there, okay?" Julia Borrows, reading with determination in the seat beside Bill, didn't even glance up. Bill gave Gurney a wink. "When we're anywhere near the Generals, we call it Myanmar."

"I'll just have to be quiet," she answered.

"They should have named you pitta. Like the pitta of little feet," Bill said.

"I've seen that bird," Ivan said. 'The Gurney's Pitta. I think I have. One of the last times I was in Burma. I'm pretty sure. It was a very rare bird anyway," Ivan got sillier by the moment, the way men often did around Gurney. "Very pretty bird."

The next time Robert looked up, Ivan was going on with something about "exploratory research" and "various American interests" and Bill had turned back around in his seat. The plane was just out of Chicago, another seventeen hours to go.

"They hire me because I speak so many languages. You really need Asian languages for clothing manufacture. I've got more connections in Thailand, but Burmese labor is the better bargain."

Gurney was getting sleepy, unfocused, and Robert worried that Ivan could misinterpret the expression in her beautiful eyes. He jiggled around to distract them, made a big project out of wiping his hands with a Wet Nap, but Ivan went on and on.

Robert flipped through the flight magazine. Visit Chicago! Visit Singapore! He dumped the magazine and went back to his laptop, trying to ignore all the distracting starts and stops of Ivan and Gurney's conversation.

"'The problem with third world countries," Ivan was going strong, "is they put on a good show while you're there, but who knows what they do the minute you leave?" Ivan plunked the call button. Ivan was wrestling to undo his seatbelt. "So, what's your business in Burma?"

"My parents were lost there ten years ago. But I never found their bodies, or anything, I mean, I saw my father get killed. I did see that."

"Don't you think that's more than Ivan needs to know?" Robert said.

"Poor Gurney," said Ivan.

"I hope to visit the plateau area where my mother was last seen. The Ting Hill monastery," Gurney said. Robert elbowed her. "And this is my husband Robert here, that's his boss and his wife." Gurney gestured to the Borrows both faking asleep now in front of them. "We're like a business group."

"Does Dramamine work differently on women?" Robert asked her. "You are so talkative. I thought the Dramamine would make you sleepy." And Robert whispered, "Can you practice appropriate? We are representing investors, major investors and you sound troubled." He didn't mean to say that. "Nut," he revised. "Wild child," he added with a chuckle, in case Ivan was overhearing, and also, Robert didn't know how he was managing to ruin his chances for sex so early on this vacation.

"Sometimes being a wild nut is a good thing," she said, batting her eyes at him. "Right?"

"In the right context," he said, and squeezed her hand.

Legroom was cramped even in first class, but they all appreciated their six extra inches out loud, and dinner was served with stainless steel instead of plastic forks. The coffee tasted strongly of soap. Robert pressed his call light. The drone of the engines was deafening at this altitude. As their bodies received doses of x-ray radiation, and collective passenger viruses ventilated, the world turned and carbon was spewed into the environment, a young Irish-looking girl (who hoped someday to become a make-up artist) made her way towards Robert.

"Excuse me," Robert said. "The coffee tastes like soap."

The stewardess uncurled her red manicure between Robert's face and her chest, took the cup, sniffed it, and gave it back.

She said. "I guess there's soap in it." She reached overhead for a pillow, passed it to Ivan. Robert studied the make-up line under her chin.

"I'd get you another cup," she said, "but it will taste the same."

Ivan said, "I thought it was pretty good," and he sucked in his cheeks, elevated his eyebrows, gave her an upside-down grin.

Slivers of Bill and Julia Borrows wiggled for circulation, the tops of their heads, pieces of pillows and reading materials, kept appearing and disappearing in front of them. Robert's legs were starting to swell.

"I'll just have the tomato juice."

"Someone in economy class must be having an embolism about now," Gurney said.

Robert was forced to listen to Ivan laugh.

Gurney said, "Hopefully it's someone high up in the Myanmar military."

"Neh, neh," Ivan said. He had a snorty laugh.

"I'm not joking. They travel you know. They go on vacation in New York. I wonder if they travel first class." Gurney looked around, "Oops."

"Gurney," Robert whispered. "Be careful. "

"For God's sake Robert, we're on an airplane. I'm just having silly conversation, trying to have fun. What else is there to do?"

He looked at his hands, twiddled his thumbs.

They flew on in boring, eardrum-pounding pressure for some time. The air vent blew in their faces as a man in the back of the plane had a terrible coughing fit. Up and down the aisle, they took turns stretching legs, wiggling feet one at a time, hanging onto the tops of the upholstered seats.

Finally, the plane landed, and taxied to the gate.

"Fish curries, fruit pastes, rice wine," Bill said. "And there's a swimming pool at the hotel."

"I hope my beautiful young wife brought a bikini bathing suit," Robert said.

"No, no," she said. 'That would offend the local customs. We all go naked here."

"Glad to know." The adventure started to feel like fun.

Once out of customs, the heat and clamor of Yangon hit them along with shouts from a horde of taxi drivers, who waved from behind a guarded barrier. The Generals were in uniform, just in front of the barriers, holding up a misprinted sign: "Welcome Ballows."

Julia had one of her laughing fits, grabbed Gurney's arm, and just managed to suppress it. "It appears our company name was somehow lost in translation," she whispered.

"I made most of my arrangements by phone," Bill said.

"Mr. Ball-ohs, Mr. White, good to meet you! And your lovely wives." They all bowed heads slightly, and the Generals

(Representatives of the Myanmar Development Council, General Than Te Ne and General Peter Ho) shook their hands. A white van pulled up to the sidewalk with its capsule of air-conditioned air, and they all packed in. A clutch of trishaws, over-stuffed cars, pickup trucks, bicycles, and motorbikes was backed up behind a trio of horse-drawn taxis.

General Ne warned them from the sidewalk, "It's rush hour." Gurney and Robert braced themselves. "We'll meet back at the hotel."

A two-wheeler gas mini-bike passed the van with four passengers aboard: a man driving, two women sidesaddle, and a baby in between.

"Look at that," Borrows said, seeing the same thing from the back seat.

More scooters with driver and sidesaddle passengers, several taxis, a small truck, and dozens of bicycles passed.

"I never knew it was possible to fit so much onto a bike," Borrows said.

Gurney twisted her hair into a scarf, stuffed her sweater into her backpack, and stared out the window. Horse-drawn taxis had stopped at the edge of a public market, blocking the road. The van's driver honked, rolled down his window, and drove up around them onto a curb. Julia slapped her hands up to cover her eyes. Pedestrians stared into the van's windows from six inches away. The bumped back onto the road.

Buddhist shrines covered the city sidewalks, adorned with wilted flowers, beads, tiny bottles of shampoo and other offerings, competing for space with vendors, pedestrians, feral dogs, women operating treadle sewing machines. An odd-looking crew of women, children, and men was grading dirt, dumping gravel, and raking asphalt from buckets onto the beginnings of a new section of road.

Robert said. "Are those little kids working on the road?"

Gurney took her husband's hand, gave it a squeeze. "That's how they pay taxes."

Guards waved the van to outside barricades, and their bags rattled with items Gurney had collected to donate to a refugee camp: anti-malarial medications, pencils, mosquito repellent. Gurney leaned her head against Robert's shoulder. They were all tired.

"That's cute," Bill was sitting behind them now.

"Doesn't he ever get tired?" Gurney whispered.

Robert reached an arm around Gurney and closed his eyes. The sun was setting as they rattled over old pavement and sections of rubble road, and finally, bumped up onto newer asphalt. They sped the last half-mile to a very contemporary looking 200-room hotel where the sign read "Best Asian" in neon English and was underlined with five stars. It was a monolith, built of brick and cement and backed up against Inya Lake. Bill exclaimed with relief when he saw it.

"Looks like you'll be able to buy a burger," Gurney said.

Bill stretched out of the van. "And flies," he gave his bucktoothed impersonation of Jerry Lewis. "Bugga an flies."

Julia tipped their smiling driver with a US dollar.

Bill held out his hand to steady his wife and then held out a hand for Gurney too. Robert almost fell out of the van. "My legs are wobbly," Robert apologized to the driver, and gave him a twenty.

"We need to change our money," he said aloud, "as soon as we get into the hotel."

Porters piled their luggage high on a trolley, and paraded it past teak and glass doors to a gleaming stone and brass reception desk. The hotel was nearly empty and smelled of fresh paint. The swimming pool was drained (or hadn't been filled yet); the carpet was plush and clean, black with tufted red roses, and gold stems, mirrors lined the walls. Everything was more Chinese looking than Burmese.

The women who greeted them had eyes outlined in black, and red mouths outlined in white, hair pinned high on their heads, flowers behind their ears. They filled out paperwork and porters led them to their rooms.

Gurney yawned, her eyes watered. The Borrows were bumping luggage across the hall. Robert and Gurney entered their room, got rid of their porters, and slammed the door. Robert gave her an evil grin. "I'm prepared to give you a quick head to toe massage. How's about that?"

Borrows rapped on the door. Robert had to open it.

"Freshen up, we'll have our drink with the Generals." It was not a question.

"Not me," Gurney said. "I'm not paid to do that," and she pointed to a tiny refrigerator that held several bottles of water and wine and beer and candy bars already in their room.

Borrows squinted at her. "'Well then you come down, Robert," he said, "that's considered polite. And you," he looked at Gurney, "can start tomorrow morning." And he left them alone.

Gurney waited for the bath to fill, resting on the bed with a pillow under her legs.

"I'm tired," she told Robert. "I just need to be quiet for a little while."

He stretched out on the mattress beside her, stuffed a pillow under his legs too, and took her hand.

When the tub was almost full, she pulled off her clothes, mostly ignoring him, poured shampoo into the running water so that it frothed.

She asked, "Aren't you going to meet with Bill? "

"I want to watch you float," he said. A bubble bath is the sort of thing Robert never did on his own, but Robert liked her bubble baths. "I thought I'd wait for you."

"But I'm not going," she said, and climbed into the tub, leaned back, closed her eyes, breasts shining between the suds like islands of a new world. "Can you bring me back something?" she asked. "The Bangkok Post? I'd really like to just rest and think for a little while. How do you keep going?"

Since he didn't know what else to do, he put his shoes and jacket back on. He was exhausted. "We'll be downstairs, then, at the bar," he said.

"I know. I'm not going anywhere."

Julia and Bill were sitting with the Generals.

"Good evening, Good evening! Nekayoyayla!" There were more employees in the bar than customers. "Wonderful to have our friends from Merger Gas visit us again."

"This is Mr. White's first time," Borrows said.

"Do I remember meeting you before?" One of the Generals looked at Bill Borrows, a confused expression on his face.

"Well, I met you the first time when I was working for ARCO. But that was some time ago. Now, we work for Merger."

"I see."

Robert said, "My wife had to rest, but she looks forward to meeting you."

General Ho balanced on his heels and smiled warmly. "Of course."

Bill was sucking down some kind of fruit drink.

"...and all Merger Gas really needs to see," Robert eventually added, striking what he hoped was an informal yet authoritative tone, "is that working conditions meet our overseas standards, or that they can be made to meet our standard. Also that the environment, of course, is being protected to the extent of our overseas standard." Bill Borrows had given Robert a booklet that detailed Merger Gas overseas standards, and he'd been trying to understand it for days.

"And that shouldn't be difficult," Borrows assured them all. "Merger Gas is hands-on. We like to visit our investments personally, get to know our host country, and be good neighbors."

"Myanmar is a very small country," General Ho said, "with primitive technology. For example, elephants."

"I love elephants," Julia remarked.

"We're not animal rights activists," Bill qualified. "We won't have any problem with the way you use elephants, I'm sure."

"But we'd like to see it," Julia added.

The General chuckled. "We take very good care of our elephants. We will take you out to see pipeline as soon as possible. You will find it interesting to watch the elephants work. There's quite a bit of progress since our last inspection, Mr. Borrows. Do you remember when that was?"

Borrows coughed, "It has been some time, hasn't it?"

"More than a year," the General pressed him to guess.

Bill Borrows' eyes watered, "April, 2008."

The Generals smiled. "Correct." The room was quiet. Julia looked at Robert. It was his turn to say something, but Julia said, "I'd love to ride in one of those horse carts."

"You will ride in a horse cart!" The Generals spoke together for a moment in Burmese, and then General Than Te Ne spoke. "We will meet in the lobby each evening, to plan the itinerary for the next day."

Q: What did the Buddhist say to the hot dog vendor?

A: Make me one with everything

16. The Death Threat January 18, 2000

Since September 7, the first day of school, Bobby worried that Hugh Moran was going to kill him. That's practically six months, he told himself. Six months, and I've had someone after my life.

"What are you, a faggot today?" Rickie asked.

Bobby tried to make it obvious that he absolutely wasn't a faggot, but his hair had grown longish, and today under an enormous trench coat he was wearing a formal shirt, suspenders, and stripped wool pants.

As far as best friends go, Rickie was annoying. A seventh grader who saw himself as an expert on Middle School, Rickie warned Bobby when his vocabulary was uncool, when his sandwich was disgusting, and when his appearance was fag-like.

"Pray you don't run into the Moron dressed like that. He's waiting for you to wear suspenders, so he can twist them around your neck."

With a head the size, shape and color of a loaf of oatmeal bread, Hugh Moran denned exactly eight houses away, and was the worst possible sort of sixth-grader, having stayed back for two years. Whenever kids talked about Hugh Moran behind his back, it was usually in the context of how they might defend themselves, and they referred to him as "Huge Moron." All last summer, in fact, Bobby thought "moron" was his real last name. But on the first day of sixth grade, the homeroom teacher asked Bobby to call attendance. It was an assignment she'd give to a different kid every school day for the entire year, and there'd never be another kid who called out "Hugh moron" and fully expected Hugh to say "Here."

"Where're you going?"

"School." Bobby said.

The last thing in the world he was going to admit to Rickie was that he was wearing the base layer of what would later become (with the addition of a cape and hat) a wizard costume for the school play. Rickie was not the sort of guy who participated in after school activities, or who got the role of Wizard of Oz, and it seemed best not to mention that Bobby was.

It was weird having his parents gone. Good in some ways, not so good in others. When his mother was around, she embarrassed him, told him stuff to do, asked him about his life. But also, when his mother was around, she walked him home. And lately, it was Rickie walking him home. Bobby liked to hang out with Rickie, but maybe not quite so much.

And also, he wanted to tell his parents about the on-going problem with Hugh Moran. But he didn't want to worry his mother. She'd freak. She'd want to talk to Hugh's dad again, because instead of getting over it (as his mother had predicted last summer), Hugh had killing Bobby on his personal "to do" list.

Fortunately, Bobby didn't run into Hugh very often. In fact, by the time his parents left for Myanmar, Bobby had practically forgotten to look both directions before he ran down the street. But now, a threat was hanging over his entire new semester schedule. Hugh was everywhere, they even shared classes, and it was four more days until his parents came home. Rickie was the only one who might come to his rescue, and Rickie liked to cause trouble, more than solve it.

Sunday, Rickie broke bottles on the curb of Commonwealth Avenue, waited to see if a car would pull over and pop a tire. They slowed down, but they didn't pull over and stop.

On their walks to school, Rickie often played "Anarchist," which meant, smash a bottle, and punch the air while shouting "Anarchist? Hell Yeah!" He did it a lot.

"Hey Rickie," Bobby asked, stepping over the most recently smashed bottle. "What's anarchist mean again?"

"Fuck the pollution! Fuck the fucking cars! Fuck the fucking assholes!"

Rickie turned thirteen last July 28, but he was only one grade higher than Bobbie in school. He pulled a cigarette out of his jacket pocket, and lit it up. "It's like a political party, a religion, sorta." Rickie was calmer when he was smoking.

Bobby thought maybe Rickie was making the word "anarchist" up. He wanted to ask someone how it was spelled, look it up if it was real, but first he wanted some assurance that using the word wouldn't make him look like an idiot.

"A nark." Rickie said. "A, nark, ist. You know. Those guys dressed in black with the big guns. Freedom fighters. They're part of the Republican Party. The rebel part."

"Oh."

"It started out in England I think."

They were on the sidewalk heading into the wind, walking toward Hill Middle School in Cambridge. It was a bitter cold 9 degrees; the sidewalks were slick with ice, the roads gritty with sand. Cold air dried their nostrils and sucked the warmth out of their hands and feet and faces.

The city was different in the winter; everyone seemed so bundled up and sealed off from one another. The fog of frozen breath mixed with Rickie's cigarette, whirled around them, Rickie coughed. Last year, Rickie caught pneumonia.

Slipping on a patch of dirty sidewalk ice, they scrambled up a short bank of snow near the cross walk, looked both ways, scrambled back down and crossed the road together. Rickie liked to wave the cigarette around, especially when they were crossing a street. Now his hands were beet red from the cold, and so he stomped it out, stuffed his hands in his pockets, searching for Tic Tacs.

"Aren't you worried about your mother," Bobby asked, "Catching you with a cigarette?"

"Nah, she smokes. What's she gonna say?" Rickie dug out a package of Tic Tacs and was trying to open it. "My fingers are swollen," Rickie told Bobby, "Can you get this for me?"

Cinnamon flavor. Their breath steamed and Bobby quietly pretended to exhale smoke. He'd tried smoking a cigarette once, and hated it, but it was still fun to pretend.

The school was at the top of this road. The crossing guide was up there, waving cars past the drop-off point.

"Who told you?" Bobby asked.

"That she smokes? What do you mean? I catch her all the time. She sneaks them out the back door."

"No, I mean about Hugh. That he's going to kill me."

"Hugh did, man. He says it every time I see him. He goes, 'that faggot friend of yours? I'm gonna kill him.'"

The boys were stomping past the brick entrance to the school.

"I'll walk you home if you want. Meet me here after school," Rickie said, and they clumped into the main hall, snow boots leaving clods of muddy ice in a path behind them. "Maybe we can do something."

Bobby nodded his head, but he had drama after school. He wouldn't say anything to anybody. He'd walk home by himself.

Rickie pulled off his book bag, and dug a package of tissues out of the inner compartments. "Dude," he said, "You've got boogers."

"I know," Bobby said, "I don't care," and he ran the last few steps to a bathroom, to wipe off his face off where no one was watching.

Isaiah 40: The voice said, Cry. And he said, "What shall I cry? All flesh is grass."

17. Meditation

January 18, 2000

People were sick; mosquitoes were up your nose and in your eyes. Army of God made them to move camp every few days, which was safer, but it's exhausting to keep moving, you wind up hungry and dirty and sick. Thailand turned back anyone who couldn't prove they were from the Karen or Karenni tribes, so their group (once nearly fifteen men, and twice as many women and children) got sick and died and was killed or lost, one by one by one. Some women and men were arrested and put into labor camps. The young men joined resistance forces. Children died, disappeared. All that was left of their original group were Sister Rita, Mya, a few younger women, four children.

Many women suffer like this, looking for lost pieces.

She told Rita, as well as she could, what she remembered about two children. She remembered a son, a daughter, and a husband. She had no faces in her mind, just the weight of them. She didn't know if she was Karen or Karenni. Rita said she'd find out what she could.

Falling from one universe into another, remembering nothing of the past: every birth is like this. But she remembered some things. Songs, for one. Little sayings. Bathing, she inspected her body for signs of motherhood. Her nipples were large and her pale belly soft with silvery stretch marks. She looked for proof that she had a child. They'd be grown now. Her hands were wide hands, with tapered fingers. A musician's hands. She meditated: my mother's hands, my father's hands, my hands, my children's hands.

Life suspends us all, throws us into orbit.

The children stayed tiny, and were hungry all the time. Right now, three of them (two girls, one boy) were pretending to ride an elephant, swaying, sitting quietly on the ground. They were very good, quiet children.

Porters and rebels and refugees were bringing in food and medicine. Naw, the littlest, was doing her washing with Mya at the stream. A bird was singing. Earlier, God's Army soldiers had scooped a cup of rice out of the bag for Mya, and she had cooked it and shared it with Naw.

Washing her head, smoothing the bristles of her hair, a melody of birds, river water, rustling leaves and mosquitoes hummed. Now, Naw's mother was dead too. Mya washed and

175

squeezed water out of Naw's hair, used her sleeve to wipe a dribble of mud off Naw's eyebrow.

"Paw Nyunt!" Naw said, and pointed down the road.

Paw Nyunt and his elephant Bago had been visible all morning in the gorge, dragging logs from the mountain. Peering through a screen of branches, now Mya noticed something she'd never seen there before. Men in Western clothes, and many more in military uniforms, were on the other side of the river. Her heart jumped. She caught herself thinking, "they've finally come for me."

But they hadn't come for her. They were taking Paw Nyunt's elephant.

Q. How many anarchists does it take to change a light bulb?

A. None, the light bulb must change itself. All anarchists can do is help its process of self-change.

18. Explosives January 19, 2000

Hugh and Rickie and Bobby shared multi-age art studio for three weeks. Hugh Moran held up a clay-carving tool, checking the sharpness of the edge, then he looked right at Bobby and giggled. Chills ran down Bobby's spine.

Art studio was Bobby's favorite and he wasn't going to let Hugh Moran wasn't going to ruin it for him. This teacher was also his favorite. You could talk to Mr. Hunt about anything, from Hitler to armpit hair.

"The assignment was to bring something 'emblematic' to class." Almost anything, including computer-generated graphics, fashion, toys, and movies, was allowed.

So Bobby held up Ricky's box of Tic Tacs.

"Shaped like pills," Bobby said. "That's weird when you think about it."

Half the class was rummaging through backpacks now, pulling out gum and candy wrappers.

"How'd you get my TicTacs?" Ricky said.

Hugh Moran banged on his desk. "Can I have a Tic-Tac?"

"It's kind of like a pill bottle," Bobby said. "Like, fake medicine."

Kids started to pull out packaging as though they'd planned for this, Mr. Hunt displaying boxes and wrappers in and out of direct light, in front of different backgrounds, and they talked about what the packaging might represent.

Bobby loved this kind of stuff, loved feeling part of the whole conversation going on below the surface of everyday life. Then Mr. Hunt started laughing at one of Penny's cartoons. She wouldn't show her cartoons to anyone but Mr. Hunt.

"Let me see that!" Hugh made his way across the room.

"Not a chance, sport," Mr. Hunt said, clapped a hand onto Hugh's shoulder and smiled him back to his table. Bobby made a mental note to run to Mr. Hunt's room if Hugh tried to kill him while at school.

Karen Rafferty raised her hand, and held up a poster of a clenched fist.

"Black and white!" Mr. Hunt exclaimed. "What does that symbolize?"

"Well, my mother is an anarchist, and anarchists don't like to pay for color posters. So, she had to make it black and white."

"Wow," Bobby gasped, and Karen looked in his direction, so much red pouring into her face that she didn't seem able to sit back down, but she hung onto her braid like a lifeline. "Anarchists?" he asked. "That means…"

Rickie was squirming noisily in his seat at the back of the room. "Kill off the rich evil bastards and rule yourself!" Rickie jutted one fist in the air.

"Okay Rickie, ignoring the language and focusing on the message, that sounds like a complaint? Could anarchism be saying, "I don't want to get bossed around by an elite ruling class?" Does that sound right?"

"Yeah," Rickie said. "Rich people think they're better than everybody else."

Bobby felt a roller coaster glide around his gut. It wasn't the way he talked, or dressed, or thought, or the way he made a mistake pronouncing Moran. It was that Bobby had new sneakers, a new backpack, new sweats. That pissed off Hugh, too. Bobby's family had money.

Hugh added, "We don't need some big-ass snot-faced rich-dude rule!"

Rickie sang out, "Anarchists forever! Yeah!"

179

At the end of the day, Rickie wasn't waiting for Bobby, and in spite of the fact that Bobby had planned and schemed for this, he found himself wiping his nose with his sleeve, batting back tears clumping on his eyelashes. Wizard of Oz rehearsal ran late, and now it was dark out, bitter cold, starting to snow. He'd never walked home all by himself before. He kicked at a clump of snow with his boot.

If Hugh and Rickie are waiting down the street, Bobby hoped and dreaded as he trudged along, I'm dead meat.

The phone rang. Desmond was in the kitchen. "Desmond? Is Bobby there?" It was Gurney.

"Sorry," Desmond said. "It's four in the afternoon here."

"Here, it's the middle of the night. I couldn't sleep. How's the weather?"

"Blizzard."

"It's hot here."

"Are you okay?" Desmond asked.

Gurney's voice sounded small and distant, as though she was holding the phone too far under her chin. "It's a completely frustrating trip. We haven't been able to get out of the city. And I'm not sleeping well." She faded in and out. "We've seen Inya Lake. We've gone shopping. We've gone to

cemeteries. We've gotten drunk." Gurney's voice dropped."
Bill keeps trying to get me to help him with that sideline thing
he's got going, and he's mad that I won't. And his connections
are all evaporating. We don't have a driver."

Desmond said, "Speak into the receiver. Did you call
Maung Ye?"

"Bill told us not to. He said the last thing Maung Ye
needs is a bunch of white people from Borrows Inc. knocking
on his door. And I don't want to attract attention to anyone
who doesn't need attention." She was almost whispering.

"You've got your MERGER Gas letter, right?" Desmond
said. "That's a good smoother-over. And you're sure Maung
wrote that note, about Maung Ye, right?"

"Yes," Gurney said. "I'm sure."

"Then, Maung wants you to call Maung Ye."

"But what if I find him? What do I do then?"

Desmond said, "Remember that other person you used
to be? That brave young girl?"

Gurney said, "I was never brave."

"Wicked brave," he told her. "Impressively brave."

"Desmond. I will try."

"Don't try," Desmond said. "Just give the guy a call. See
what he says."

Gurney's voice got louder. "And Desmond, do you mind, picking Bobby up at school? It's dark now so early."

"No problem whatsoever," Desmond said. He braced himself to contend with driving again in this weather. "We're having a great time. I was just getting ready to go pick him up."

"As a rule, human rights groups do not have direct access to on-scene information in [Burma]. We do." Merger Gas Report to Shareholders

19. Karmic Debt

Yangon, Burma January 23, 2000

They were finishing off breakfast, frustrated. During the day, their military escorts (Gurney called them "guards") didn't speak a word of English. Evenings, they suffered through meals listening to upper echelon Myanmar military men justify the finer points of dictatorship.

For example in America, they said, you pay taxes. But in Myanmar, money isn't so easy to come by, so civilians work for the common good. The Generals used up three evenings explaining why this, or any variation of this, shouldn't be confused with forced labor.

"But what if you're a farmer, and you already have more work than you can do? What if it's harvest time, or planting time?"

"You pay someone else to do your labor," the Generals explained.

"But what if you can't afford to do that?"

General Than Te Ne didn't like questions, and his manner with Gurney became strained. "The same thing that happens in your country when you don't pay your taxes. Pay taxes, or go to prison!"

"Honey, he's right," Robert said, "This is very similar to our country!" He rubbed his head, and found the idea of working with a dictatorship impossible to digest.

And Gurney was semi-hysterical as well. "People go hungry," she said, but the Generals got up to get more coffee.

"Maybe they don't know what the word 'hungry' means either," Julia said.

Bill said, "Certainly not at this buffet." He pushed out his chair from the table. "At least I'm not hungry."

Julia said, "Count your blessings."

After breakfast, the Generals and even the guards disappeared for a while. Borrows held a huddle to plan out what they'd do next. The pipeline project had run into some sort of a problem, Bill guessed. The Generals were stalling to keep them from seeing it, and in only four days, Borrows Inc. would be going back to Boston.

"All I'm asking Gurney, is for you to help me cultivate a few social connections for the next time we visit. Just talk to this guy on the phone."

"I don't like the sound of your friends, Bill," Gurney was adamant.

Robert was embarrassed. "I don't understand what you're fighting about," Robert said.

"I'm going to make a phone call," Gurney said, rummaging through her bag. "I have the number of a driver who can bring us out there."

"Blame it on me," Robert approved, surrendered. He was tired, suffering culture shock, couldn't even think in his usual way.

"I'm staying here," Bill told them.

Robert said, "Don't you need to see the pipeline?"

Borrows said, "MERGER has to send another team out in April or May anyway. "

Robert said, "You look like you've got malaria, for God's sake."

Borrows laughed, "Nah," he said, "It's this heat!"

"But it should be okay for us to go out to the pipeline?" Julia unwrapped a piece of gum, folded it into her mouth. "That's not breaking any big rules. Right?"

Bill replaced his glasses, rubbed the corners of his mouth. "I think so."

"Careful Bill," Gurney told him.

"Don't worry," he said. "Go inspect. That's a good thing."

"That must be Maung Ye," Gurney said, and she took Robert's arm. Maung Ye's truck was pulling up in front of their hotel half an hour after she called.

"Okay!" Maung Ye said, "Hello!" Maung Ye looked about forty years old. Maung Ye spoke English with a British accent, took their backpacks, put them in the back. All the waiting around had been driving Julia and Gurney crazy, so they climbed into the front seat immediately.

"Sorry we can't all ride up front," he apologized to Robert. "Are you okay back here?"

Robert tried to get comfortable resting against their backpacks. An open window divided the cab from the truck bed and Robert positioned himself to hear their conversation.

Maung Ye was saying, "I heard so much about you! Good for you! To leave Burma, and come back, with fresh views!" Gurney denied having done anything good, but Maung Ye went on. "Sometimes in Burma, we feel like the forgotten people." A strand of fresh flowers swung from the mirror of his truck, infusing the air with a lemony scent.

"I've never forgotten," Gurney said.

Maung Ye started the engine. "The exhaust system!" He shouted back to Robert, "Sorry!"

Bill came round to the back of the truck. "Here," he said and passed Robert an envelope. "Now don't lose that. That's your letter of introduction. It's very, very important."

"Thanks," Robert said.

"I'm going back to entertain at the bar, hand out American cigarettes and see if I can get lucky with the waitress. Kidding. Hey. Be careful." Bill squinted. A bicycle driven by a middle-aged man tooled past, splashed up a puddle.

Maung Ye released the clutch, and they drove through the city, past suburban rice fields, and into the hills. Bouncing around in the back, Robert tried to focus on the fine print of the letter Borrows had given him. "Authorizing and identifying Bill Borrows, Julia Borrows, Robert White, Gurney White, as MERGER GAS staff personnel in Myanmar with authority to enter and inspect the pipeline site and related facilities. Issued by MERGER GAS."

It could have been signed by someone from Merger Gas, he thought, and searched for a company seal. It would have been nice if the authorization had been co-signed by the Generals.

"...Seven years, and in solitary confinement for three years..."

"What are you saying?" Robert hollered.

Maung Ye shouted back over the muffler's racket. "Two years ago, they finally let me go! I was 32 years old then. Ha! ha, ha, ha!"

"Why is he laughing?" Robert asked his wife.

"What else is he supposed to do?" She shook her head.

"And Maung Naing was in prison with me too," Maung Ye said.

The fumes in the back of the truck and the need to see the expression on his wife's face forced Robert to lean towards the partition.

"Everybody loves him. He's a very inspiring poet," Maung Ye said.

"He's alive?" Robert asked.

Maung Ye went on, "We both were sent to Insein in 1990, and they let us out almost the same time, 1997. We made bricks together. He made it bearable, singing poetry in my ear. But they arrested Maung again, kept him till last spring. That was bad. It's awful what they did to him."

"What did they do?" Gurney inhaled the question.

"They made him stand in a bucket for two weeks, poking him with a cattle prod." Maung Ye drove with both hands on the wheel. "Maung hasn't been the same since that."

Maung Ye swerved around a truck broken down on the side of the road, and Robert banged his head. "But I didn't hear from him again until I saw his picture in the paper last summer. Remember when Righteous Burmese Warriors took over Myanmar Embassy?"

"They took hostages," Gurney said.

"Right," Maung Ye said. "Maung Naing was there."

Gurney's neutral expression evaporated, "I doubt that."

"No mistake," Maung Ye said.

Gurney held the dash with one hand. "Maung wouldn't take hostages."

"But he was there," Maung Ye said calmly. "And then Thailand expelled them all from the country." The truck rumbled across a bridge. On either side of the stream, weedy rice fields stretched for hundreds of acres. Water buffalo waded on the edges.

"The last message I got from Maung came from Bangkok," Maung Ye said. "He joined God's Army there."

"God's Army?"

189

"They helped us last October and November, clearing landmines. But they're not doing that now. They are trying to raise money for food and medicine. They want Thailand to help. At least, that's the rumor." Maung Ye patted the steering wheel.

"How?"

"I am sorry to tell you. They have taken over a Bangkok Hospital."

"Right now? Is Maung there?"

"Yes. I believe so. They are holding hostages again."

Gurney folded her hands together, and was making a steeple, tapping it to her lips, staring over the dash as the rice fields dropped away from the road. "We need to go to Bangkok!"

Maung Ye said, "Not yet. Maung asked me to bring you back to Ting Hill." He smiled at Gurney. "He is asking you to take photographs. He wants you to check with the nuns, as one of them may be your mother."

Exhaust was so bad in the back, Robert was dizzy and sick, his face pressed into the cab partition. His back hurt, he needed air.

Gurney said, "My mother was staying at Ting Hill when it was attacked. I was told there were no survivors."

Maung Ye tapped on the wheel, "There were some survivors."

"What's this?" Robert asked, but Maung Ye didn't respond.

"What?" Robert hollered. "I can't hear. What?"

"But Gurney, many people learn English, they dream of getting into the United States. If they have any connection, anything at all, they cultivate it. They don't forget. I personally don't believe this is really your mother. But she might have known your mother. She might have known you."

Robert fell back from his porthole and tried to rest his eyes without passing out.

They came upon a group of ragged children huddled in the dust at the side of the road, playing a game, serious faces shining out from under dark sparkling hair. A row of shacks, and a pack of dirty white dogs, bright clothes in different sizes all hung over a muddy yard with weathered, unfinished construction looming up here and there. The truck bumped along. Gurney said, "This road isn't shown on the map." The truck hit a pothole; they all hit the ceiling. Robert nearly got tossed out.

Then the buildings were gone, the truck groaned through more ruts and puddles, and they hit a paved stretch through the middle of nowhere that went about a mile. An animal carcass was on the side of the road, and a blur of color slipped away from it like a shadow as they passed.

The road degraded again. They creaked up and down a dozen more miles until it became impassable and Maung Ye shut off the engine. Snake grass and a tangle of vines brushed against the truck. A breeze was blowing up. They were nearly on top of a limestone precipice over a stream.

"Crahht!"

They heard something between a bark and a yowl with overtones of a scream.

"Tiger," Maung Ye said.

"Really?" Robert looked around. "Doesn't sound very far away."

"She probably doesn't want to meet us any more than we want to meet her," Maung Ye said.

Julia picked up a rock. "I never heard a tiger roar before," she said.

Gurney exclaimed, and pointed beyond the ravine towards a distant place where the earth seemed to bend. "See over there, where it looks like a giant's knee?"

Robert looked, expecting to see the animal. "No."

"That right there. That's Ting Hill."

The air was cooler and sweeter here, translucent, full of moisture, mixing sun and sky and infinite shades of green.

Robert told his wife, "You look so beautiful when you smile, you should smile more often."

"I'm sorry I haven't been smiling," she said.

They opened water bottles, swatted mosquitoes, listened for the tiger, but didn't hear it again.

Robert touched Gurney's narrow shoulder, held out his hand, pulled her up. "I'm ready," he said, "Let's go."

No inspector wants to find problems. The dictatorship didn't want Robert to find problems; Merger Gas didn't want him to find problems; Bill Borrows didn't want him to find problems. There was a gnawing at the pit of Robert's stomach, a dread of the problems they would surely find. They left the truck parked under a tree in a weed-tangled turnout.

"This was once a public school," Maung Ye said. "Look. All that's left," he had to dig to find it, "is this layer of ash."

"We're in the war zone," Gurney said, and she passed Robert his water bottle.

Maung Ye told them, "Stay on the trail. Keep your eyes open for landmines. Don't step on any kind of litter, especially nothing plastic or metal."

193

Robert chuckled, shook his head, said, "I don't know why I'm laughing."

Julia looked at him, aghast.

"What?" he said. "You don't think I have a right to laugh?"

"And don't wear hats, especially you Julia, and Robert." Maung Ye went on, "In case soldiers spot us, we want them to see pretty foreigner hair."

"What sort of soldiers?" Robert asked. Gurney had scrambled up a rock to peer over the ravine, and was focusing on a better view of Ting Hill.

Maung Ye said, "There are several. Let's just hope we don't get caught in between any of them."

Shadows spread, the sun got lower, and Robert's socks kept falling into his shoes. Julia had a can of mosquito repellent and they sprayed each other—arms and legs and necks. The rainforest was quiet.

"When were you in the U.S.?" Robert asked him.

"84-85. Student exchange."

Vines blocked the trail, and Maung Ye hacked them back.

Robert tried to walk without bending his feet, to compensate for the exhaustion of his shins.

"I always wanted to be the kind of monk who lived quietly in a temple, teach, ring the bells, light the incense," Maung Ye sighed. "But look at me now."

"Now you're a diplomat instead of a monk," Gurney said and Maung Ye laughed.

They slipped and stumbled over roots and rocks and slippery foliage, the trail filled with sheaves of fallen leaves, green saturating every shaft of light, glittering and reflecting off their skin with a limy scent of flower.

Gurney brushed hair out of her eyes, looped her arms through Robert and Julia's. Gurney wasn't usually this demonstrative, this affectionate.

"I wish I knew how to operate a machete," Robert said. He tried.

"You're going to cut off something important," Julia warned.

"That's okay, let me do it," Maung Ye told him, "You don't need to know how to do this. You live in Boston." The trail went up a rock outcropping; Robert and Gurney steadied each other.

"What are you smiling about?" Robert asked his wife.

"I feel happy," Gurney said.

Robert thought: Maung didn't die. What if her mother didn't die, either? What if all this time Mya Williams had simply been lost amongst the 2,000,000 refugees thought to have attempted the border into Thailand?

Gurney said, "I'm thinking about my mother. "

"Don't set yourself up," Robert warned her.

"How could I possibly do that?" she replied, and two strides later, she put his arm around her shoulder, her hand around his waist. They supported each other as they tromped. The sky rumbled. A cool breeze rushed over them. Gurney showed him goose bumps.

"It's the wind," Maung Ye said.

Big yellow roots were mounding up out of the earth like furniture over a moss rug. Maung Ye lay down with in a spot he apparently knew well and said, "Let's rest for a few moments here."

Gratefully, they dumped backpacks, dug out fruit and sandwiches and water bottles.

"Will we get back before dark?" Julia asked.

"We'd better," Robert said. "I don't really want to be laying on a bed of leaves in this jungle overnight."

"You wouldn't be alone," Maung Ye said.

They munched, tended sore spots. Maung Ye said, "Another quarter kilometer. I've arranged a meeting."

Gurney and Julia glanced at each other.

"Why are you looking at each other like that?" Robert said.

Gurney said, "I'm just nervous."

"You don't need to be nervous on my account," Robert said.

Gurney took his hand, pulled him to standing. "I'm screwing up your Merger job, I'm afraid."

"What do you mean? We're going to see the pipeline," he said, brushing off the back of his pants. "Whatever else we see."

"That's what I'm saying Robert. Do you realize where we are? I can promise you, no westerners ever get to see this neighborhood. You are going to see some shit. Merger is not going to like it when you take these pictures home. It is not going to look good to their shareholders. If I get to see my mother," Gurney hadn't appeared anywhere near crying, and suddenly, there it was. She bent over and took a breath, turned her eyes back on him. "Let's just deal with things as we go."

He tried to hug her and stroke her hair, but she pulled away, "I don't need anything special," she said. "You act like you think I'd collapse."

Robert didn't want to grovel, and Julia and Maung Ye were listening. "I've got blisters."

197

Julia said, "I wonder what the fuck Bill is up to right now."

"Keep an eye out for landmines," Maung Ye reminded them. Gurney had her camera out. They helped each other cross a little stream, holding hands. Sweat collected on their brows, ran along the sides of their faces.

"I don't understand reincarnation," Robert said.

Gurney laughed.

"I'm just asking a question while a monk is handy," Robert said.

"Everything is connected." Maung Ye said. They had to stop for a second to catch their breath.

"Crrahhhhht!"

It startled them all.

"'There it is again," Gurney said.

"Did he answer me?" Robert asked Julia.

"A wave is born, and dies," Maung Ye said, "but the ocean is constant. Your life is like that wave, rising from the sea and falling back into it, rising up again. That's reincarnation."

"Okay," Robert said.

"Like recycling," Maung Ye said.

The path was slippery. Robert walked on the edge of his shoes.

Maung Ye tapped an empty water bottle against his leg, in rhythm with the awesome guttural cough that repeated over and over.

"It's either hungry or horny," Julia said. "And I'm not thrilled with either possibility."

"It doesn't worry me," Robert said, but he took her hand.

They kept walking. "It's sort of fun, to hear it."

Finally, they found the ancient steps, one hundred thirty six steps, with the carved stone banister that clung to Ting Hill like a vein in the arm of a God.

Below, an old banana plantation crossed a wide river valley. On the temple terrace, the view took in the valley, the hills on the other side, and they could peer beyond enormous trees, and landscaped paths punctuated by ancient, strange mounds of soil, with squares of flattened ground decomposing back into jungle. There were no buildings, and the grounds were untended, but the spirit of the monastery felt completely intact.

"The main halls were there, and these were living areas," Gurney said. "I think." They walked across a well-worn stone shelf. "This was the courtyard. Oh. The Buddha's gone."

"Yes, it is a very sad loss." Maung Ye said, "But the Buddha is still in our thoughts, and there's a shrine." He led them around some trees to a conical stupa, decked with orchid blossoms.

"Who's tending that?" Robert asked.

"Down there," Maung Ye answered. "Don't you see them?"

As their eyes re-focused on the valley, they began to recognize that the row upon row was not banana or coconut plantations, but reed and leaf huts, clinging together, stretching all the way to the horizon.

Gurney took out her camera.

"Refugees," Maung Ye nodded. "When you are ten thousand or twenty thousand people, it's impossible to hide. Tatmadaw burned them out, to make way for the pipeline, but they have nowhere else to go."

"They've made a whole city out of leaves," Gurney said.

"It almost looks pretty," Julia said, and from this distance, it did. The shining foliage reflected the late afternoon blue of the sky. They caught glimpses of people fluttering from spot to spot.

"Up close, it's not so pretty. On the one hand, it's amazing what they do, how they set up schools and share essential supplies and skills, but it is all done with no clean water, no medicine, no escape from mosquitoes. The Myanmar military knows they are here, and picks away at their young men, steals them and turns them into Tatmadaw, and all the dangers of wilderness, with the misery of war and poverty and frustration are nothing compared to that loss. We're going down there. You'll see. It isn't easy to keep your soul alive in these conditions but people do."

Exhausted from the hike, Robert blinked his eyes back under control. "If I ever dare make a case, and suggest that MERGER bail out of one of the biggest natural gas deals going down in the history of Southeast Asia…" He took a breath, blew his nose, couldn't finish the thought. The blister on his heel was making it difficult even to walk in his socks.

"I wish I had some band aids," Julia said.

"Someone is supposed to meet us here," and just as Maung Ye said this, they heard a discrete tumbling of gravel and they turned their heads.

A nun with weathered, fibrous looking flesh and one good leg was hobbling towards them. She appeared both impossibly tough and also terribly tiny and vulnerable: a contradiction that caused them all to stare.

Maung Ye picked his head up off his jacket, took his feet off a rock, and jumped up, bowing, smiling. "This is she! The nun who found the shoe!"

"Shoe?" Robert asked.

Gurney's mouth was open, her eyes staring, smiling, as the nun came closer, holding out something in her hand. "It's my mother's shoe," Gurney bent to look over the nun's extended hand, ravaged with disappointment. "But this is not my mother."

None of this made sense to Robert.

Julia said, "Reminds me of that children's book, 'You're not my mother,'" and Gurney engaged in a Burmese conversation with the nun and Maung Ye.

"Anyone care to explain this to me?" Robert asked.

"Say I'm a fool," Gurney said, "and you're right." She sat on a rock, took several breaths, her hands on her chest. She held out one shaking hand, and giggled. "Look," she said. "My hands are still shaking." Her lips were blue. Robert embraced her.

The nun spoke again, her forehead lifted, her face strained and intense, her eyes steely black, and Maung Ye translated for them all with excitement in his voice.

"So, this nun is a Sister Rita, and no, she's not Gurney's mother, but she is friends with another nun, who she says *is*

Gurney's mother. I doubted it but Rita says they look very much alike. Mya is down there, and not strong enough to climb Ting Hill."

"How far away is she?" Robert asked. He watched Gurney's face, which was nodding and blossoming like a pink wet flower. "Here," he said. "Wipe those tears on me."

"It's maybe 5 kilometers, out and back," Maung Ye said. "But the trail is very steep. It will seem further."

"Let me look at your blisters," Gurney said, they all exposed blisters to Gurney. They looked bad; six holes the size and thickness of dimes. Gurney grimaced.

"Maybe if we can find something to wrap them with," she said, "Leaves or something."

But a subtle drone that had been a very distant, like the sound of flies or bees or faint music, like an Indian sitar, buzzing slowly louder and more complicated, fell out of sync, and suddenly they heard it differently and it wasn't pretty anymore, it sounded now like growling, like dirt bikes coming up the trail. Rita's entire demeanor changed, and she turned and began hobbling as fast as she could back towards the jungle.

Julia asked, "What is this? Should we be afraid?"

"No, never fear," Maung Ye said. "They'll just check papers, that sort of thing. It can be a hassle, but probably, everything will be fine."

The motors got louder.

Gurney was pulling on her shoes and fumbling, working to tie her shoelaces.

"Just wait," Robert said, "This will probably be a ride down in the truck."

"I've got to catch up with Sister Rita, I don't want to get held up here," she said.

"No, no, we should all stick together, don't you think Maung?"

"Right," Maung Ye said. He asked Robert, "You have your letter?"

They could see the tops of the soldier's heads, riding their motorbikes up the side of the mountain, leaving a cloud of dirt hanging in the air.

"Yes," Robert said.

"That's our ice breaker," Maung Ye said, and he grimly curled up the corners of his mouth and he looked tired for the first time today.

"I'm a V.I.P!" Robert said, and hoped that Bill Borrows really had done them a favor. "Luckily for us." He fanned himself with the letter. "Americans can get away with anything anyway," he grinned.

Gurney jumped up, "Okay, Robert really, we've got to say goodbye!" she said.

"I don't think that's a good idea," Julia said. "How would you get back? It might look bad."

Robert said, "They already see us."

General Peter Ho and General Than Te Ne, and five other soldiers rode up in a swirl of dust. Robert plastered a joyous welcome on his face; the women conjured something similar, but Gurney's face was a ghastly white.

"So here you are!" Peter Ho responded instinctively to the grins, and stood off his muddy machine.

"Yes! We've had a great day," Robert answered, and Julia echoed nervously, "A beautiful day," and Gurney bowed her head, more respectful than she'd been yet with the Generals.

Maung Ye was still there too, head bowed, somberly standing behind Robert.

Robert felt his way into a friendly conversation: "We wanted to go on a hike," (the Generals frowned), "...and look at the pipeline construction...ah...and here are our papers authorizing us to view and inspect the pipeline." The Generals looked at Maung Ye. Robert tried to break their gaze. "And

Merger Gas sent me all the way out here to do an inspection and I can't go back without it." Robert was still holding out the letter.

"This is very beautiful spot," General Ho finally said, and he looked around the terrace, as though speaking to the trees. The soldiers pulled their bikes, still humming, into a semi-circle, and finally shut them off. "But this is not an approved destination. You may know this," addressing Maung Ye, yet oddly, he spoke in English.

Maung bowed apologetically, breathing softly and bowed again, looking into his hands.

"Get on," General Ho commanded them to each to climb onto the back of a motorbike. Robert saw Gurney hold onto the back of her bike seat and lean away from the General. They all avoided clinging to the thin waists of the military men.

The Generals gave them a ride back in the direction they'd come, under a thick canopy of vines blocking the sun. When they got back to Maung Ye's truck, two new soldiers were leaning against it, and Maung Ye was nowhere to be seen.

Robert exclaimed, "Where is our driver? He was going to drive us back."

General Ho had a too-serious tone of voice. "We know this man. He has a criminal record. You shouldn't trust taxi drivers. He may have been taking you here to kill you, and steal your wallets."

"I'm sure you're wrong," Robert said.

"We tricked him into driving us here," Gurney said, and held up her map, marked with pen and compass points. General Ho looked at Gurney with an incredulous expression. Robert took the map, folded it into his pocket, and took his wife's hand again. Julia looked scared, so Robert held her hand too.

Robert said, "Well. I'm glad for the ride. My feet are killing me."

"Me too," Julia said. Gurney was uncharacteristically quiet. It looked like her teeth were chattering.

"Hop in," the General said. "My officer will drive you back to Yangon."

"But we want to wait for our driver," Robert dared say. "We're here for Merger Gas," he said.

General Ho told them, "In the future, we assign your driver, for your own security."

Back at the hotel, at the after-supper meeting, Gurney pestered the Generals until she boiled over. Robert had to physically restrain her. "I want to know exactly what has happened to Maung Ye!" she shouted.

"Troublemakers live in the jungle," they told her. "For your own safety, as well as national security, we cannot let you ride with troublemakers. Imagine, if you are taken hostage by rebels? How do we explain that to your people?"

They tried to go to bed, but Gurney could only beat the pillows, pull at her hair.

"We need to get to Bangkok," she told him. They tried calling Maung Ye, but he wasn't at his own number, not at the police station. Robert developed a severe headache, and had to sleep, but Gurney got up at midnight, and found a hotel employee whose cousin worked at the police station. They also told her Maung Ye wasn't brought to the district office. The warden at Insein Prison said Maung Ye wasn't there either.

In the morning, Bill Borrows banged on the door to their room, "The Bangkok Post is reporting rebel hideouts all along the pipeline were attacked last night and early this morning by Myanmarese military. And a friend in New York also called to tell me. And Thailand is supposedly bombing too. It's going on all along the river border, getting it from both sides, right where you were, in the river valley below Ting Hill."

Robert asked, feeling sick with the realization, "We spent the whole day walking into a strike zone?"

By lunchtime, United States Consuls were warning Americans in Asia to go back home. News was now reporting that in Thailand, Burmese rebels had entered a hospital, taking hundreds of hostages. The entire region was displaying signs of instability. This hostage taking was the second hostage-taking event of the past six months. Security of Americans in South East Asia could no longer be guaranteed.

20. The Lesson

Boston January 25, 2000

Desmond asked him, "How come you were at school so late?"

"You mean, was I being an idiot and doing stuff I'm not supposed to do?"

"Not really."

"Drama practice. Remember? I told you this morning. I'm the wizard."

"But I thought you'd be home by now."

"So did I."

Once home, Bobby wanted to be left alone, eat whatever, play his game boy, go to bed. But being a kid, Desmond would hassle him about homework, or ask him to pick up his room, and that annoyed him, because grown-ups do whatever they want. Desmond did whatever he wanted to do all day long.

And bad enough that Bobby already got told what to do all day long, but Desmond was preaching to him about Buddhism and meditation practice and lifestyles, and Bobby did not want to listen to advice. Not for a week, not for a day. Not ever.

For a long time, he wanted to be a racecar driver, and everyone but him hated that idea. But recently he'd been thinking (and he'd keep his new ideas to himself), something like Eminem, a musician and poet, might be cool. It could be fun to expose the stupidness of the rich, and also be rich. Once he got his own mansion and bodyguards and swimming pool, he'd give money to children living in dictatorships. He'd give it to rebels looking to overthrow corrupt governments.

Bobby did go once a year with his parents to Maple Village Monastery, a Buddhist retreat center in Vermont. Desmond was right, there was something almost cool about being Buddhist. Even though Bobby didn't like meditating, he told people he was Buddhist sometimes and talked to Rickie about it sometimes. And he'd gone to church before, and to a synagogue once too, so he knew something about other religions. But he just didn't believe in religion. The whole God thing and Easter Bunny thing and Tooth Fairy thing and Santa Claus thing all fit pretty much into the same category in Bobby's opinion, but adults take the God thing way too seriously. The idea of a little old man sitting up in the clouds watching over the world is stupid. Meditation isn't quite as stupid, but it's boring, and Bobby would rather play basketball.

Maybe happiness is genetic, Bobby thought, and I take after my parents. Bobby's parents didn't seem as cheerful as Desmond.

And anyway, maybe it's not stupid to be happy, but maybe it's not so smart either. Life on earth as we know it might well be on its way out. Democracy was nice while it lasted, but the founding fathers of the U.S.A. didn't figure on a world where people didn't give a shit. Bobby didn't know any government that wasn't corrupt. Dictators (like the Moran!) are slowly taking over the earth.

The world was ending just as his life was beginning.

Bobby went up the front steps of his house, opened the door with the key on the chain on his book bag, and dropped his bag in the hall. Desmond picked it up, hung Bobby's book bag on the hook, set their pizza on the countertop.

The house was too quiet. The photographs on the walls made him think about his Mom and Dad and what they must be seeing: temples, child soldiers, child monks. Maybe Bobby would join the army someday, maybe the marines. Or, maybe not. He just didn't know what was the right thing to do.

In countries like Myanmar, people get thrown in jail for reading the wrong book! And lots of kids there never go to school. Or if they do, they don't study art like Bobby studied art, they have to do paintings of their own stupid dictators. Bobby examined the smiles on the photographs of the kid monks. He wished he knew if they were faking anything. They were just smiling. It looked real.

Even if being a monk makes somebody happy, Bobby didn't want to be a monk because he didn't like to meditate, but maybe it was good for the monks. He watched Desmond, checked out his smile. Maybe it was real, but maybe he was faking it.

"So how was school today?" Desmond asked. Bobby opened the box of pizza and it was his favorite. Pineapple.

"Okay."

"So, the wizard thing's going pretty good?"

"Yeah," Bobby said. On two occasions, dress rehearsal and the actual performance, Bobby gets to press a button, and set off a smoke bomb, so that he and another kid, can disappear before everyone's eyes. But he didn't get to set it off yet.

The pizza was good, Bobby was starving, he wanted to eat, not talk.

"After supper, how about if you and I go meditate for a few minutes? Your mother suggested it."

"But I'm thinking about converting to Judaism," Bobby said.

'The cat was rolling on the floor by Desmond's feet. Cats always know who's going to feed them.

"Okay then," Desmond took last night's can of cat food out of the fridge, and scooped it into the cat's dish.

"No, really Desmond. Almost everyone in my school is Jewish. There's only one other Buddhist kid, that's Nye, and he was born in Cambodia. I'd rather be Jewish." Maybe later he could say he'd converted to Buddhism.

"Jewish people meditate, too."

"Plus, I'm an anarchist," Bobby tried this out, "and that actually doesn't work well with Buddhism." The clocks were gonging.

"How so?" Desmond asked.

"I'd have to accept Buddha as my leader, and anarchists don't do that."

"Anarchists don't accept rulers? The Buddha isn't a ruler. You rule yourself in Buddhism."

The easiest thing to do with Desmond is not to talk it out, because Desmond would talk forever and still make him mediate. The best thing was to just get it over with, and then Desmond would let him have his Game Boy.

"Okay," Bobby said. "Can I light the candle?"

The Buddha in this room was a nice one, smooth greenish metal, but its eyes were always looking at you, no matter where you sat.

When his parents were home, his mother sat on the futon with her legs crossed, eyes closed, candle lit. When he was little, she let him cuddle there in her lap, if he was quiet. He used to fall asleep that way, waking up when his mother rang the bell.

Bobby crossed his legs on his mother's futon, closed his eyes, and tried to focus on his breathing. This was easier than doing the dishes or cleaning his room. He'd even tell them when they got back, "I meditated with Desmond." They'd love that kind of thing.

Bobby thought maybe Desmond was asleep; he was so still, his breathing so slow and relaxed. But Bobby couldn't relax. He had butterflies in his stomach. And when he started to think about the Moran, what he really wanted to do was run down the road screaming.

"The whole idea of meditation," Desmond said this in an eerily soft voice, "is to notice what your mind is doing, and take a break from it. Like, if you notice scary thoughts, or a sad thought, just let it go for now. Pay attention to your breathing."

215

"I know," Bobby said. Desmond was annoying. Dad says he has no body hair. Bobby doesn't have body hair either.

Then he hoped his parents weren't fighting. What if she found Maung? What would Dad do about that? Or maybe Mom was meditating, maybe she was up at Ting Hill, and even though the monastery was gone there, maybe it was still somehow beautiful. Maybe she found the pool she told him about, where she and Maung hid when they were escaping. Maybe they were riding on an elephant somewhere; his parents were both pretty brave, adventurous. They loved each other. And elephants are cool. And he breathed in. Breathed out.

Desmond was ringing the bell.

Desmond reached over and patted his shoulder. The scented candle had burnt halfway down and the room smelled like a Christmas tree.

"What time is it?" Bobby asked. The room was nearly dark, just one small flicker of candlelight.

"Nearly 7:30. And there's something I still want to do tonight, a rally in Somerville. There's going to be some excellent speakers. Come with me? We can get a hot cocoa afterwards."

The butterflies in Bobby's stomach batted their wings a few times, but more slowly now. "The WTO protest?"

"Yup. You heard about it?"

"I heard they had a rally last week in Seattle, and people broke windows. Police had to use teargas." Bobby didn't want to go. "You think it's safe for a kid like me?"

Desmond laughed. "Are you kidding? Tagging along with a guy as big and powerful as me? You're 100% safe when you're with me, kid."

"What, do you carry a gun or something"

Desmond laughed. "Go use the bathroom," Desmond said, spinning in place as though he was trying to remember which direction was the door. "And I'll get my shoes on, get the car keys and my coat and we'll check it out. I'm not leaving you home alone, and I really do want to go to the rally."

"Do we have to stay a long time?"

"No more than half an hour. It's too cold out anyway."

"So, hot cocoa?"

"Absolutely."

Bobby ran upstairs to use the bathroom. Then he dashed into his bedroom, felt around under the mattress. Found the cherry bomb and pack of matches, and tucked them into his coat pocket, just in case he needed them.

217

Attention leads to immortality. Carelessness leads to death. Those who pay attention will not die, while the careless are as good as dead already.

(Buddha)

21. The Job

Burma January 24-25, 2000

"You're reminding me, in some ways, of my father."

"I've heard that before," Robert said.

"It's just surprising me. You seem so calm."

"I'm scared to death."

"Your voice isn't trembling."

"That's because I'm scared for you, not for me. I'm just trying to end this nightmare," Robert said, "and get you back where you belong." Gurney and Robert whispered together behind Robert's open briefcase. The Generals had just asked Robert a question, and he was digging for something that would look more official in his inspection notes, but all he had was a pad of paper covered with scrawl. He took it out, flipped through the pages.

"I don't know what to say. I can't say for certain."

"But did you see any human rights violations?" General Ho asked, and Bill Borrows was bobbing his head. "Did you?"

"I saw indicators," Robert said.

In the 16 hours since Maung Ye was supposedly questioned and released, Gurney and Robert had tried dozens of times to reach anyone who could confirm he was okay. "For example, Maung Ye. Where is he?"

"Maybe he's working," General Ho said. "Even criminals need to earn a living." He chuckled at Gurney. "You worry too much."

Bill had been saying for some time now that even the subtle confrontations were freaking him out. So he kept leaping to side with the Generals. "What? You think the taxi driver was your new best friend? He's got a life to live! He's somewhere eating noodles!" he said. "Of course you don't know where he is. Why should you?"

"Shut up!" Julia bitched at Bill for Gurney, who was too exhausted for it.

"But what I'd like to do now," Robert interrupted, "is focus on the bombing at the border." Robert took a sip of his water, tried for a neutral tone of voice. "And what bombings say about human rights, what the bombings mean for Merger Gas."

How is it you can be married to someone for more than a decade, and not notice how brave they really are? For the first time since the beginnings of their marriage, he amazed Gurney. He was standing up for something he believed in. He wasn't afraid of them.

Bill, on the other hand, said, "Burma shouldn't bear the responsibility when it's Thailand dropping bombs."

"But the Generals haven't denied Myanmar has also dropped bombs, and that they're working with Thailand."

"Burning the bridges here," Bill said, and it was more of a command to Robert to stop, than a question, "Aren't we?"

A euphoric, reckless rage was taking shape in the room. Julia drank coffee and said, "I'm trying to restrict myself to just listening. They're kidnappers, for chrissakes. It makes no sense to talk with them at all."

Robert waved away the laptop the Generals wanted to set up. "But we don't need to see another Power Point. Thank you." He put a hand on his stomach as the Generals disagreed, as though he felt ill, or was digesting too much food. "No, no. Put it away. We're not going to watch it. No. No. We're done. We're all set."

Gurney smiled at him, stood behind him, put her hand on his shoulder, the hair lifting up on the back of their necks, nerves tingling in the backs of their knees. They all wanted this meeting to end. As soon as they could get a flight, they were going to Bangkok.

Bill was rumpled and sweaty as though he'd slept all day in his suit and been hauled to dinner against his will and said, "We're all rather tired." His hair was greasy and flattened.

General Ho said, "Let us show you evidence. We have it on video. Rebels cause many problems in Myanmar, many problems even with international relations. Yesterday, Burmese rebels invaded a Thai hospital! Imagine!"

"I can't imagine that," Bill said. "That's terrible, truly very terrible."

General Ho said, "Of course, we bomb! Imagine. If Canadian rebels took over Boston hospital. The USA would attack the rebel base, even if it was in Canada!"

Julia explained, "Not quite, we only attack when oil is involved."

"But if they were Mexican rebels," Robert began and Gurney completed his sentence, "Why bomb when you can suck an economy dry?"

General Ho didn't understand English terribly well, and was ignoring almost everything they said. "Thailand and Myanmar are working together, of course!"

"Myanmar and Thailand are bombing helpless people!" Gurney stood up, threw up her hands, knocked over her coffee, all but shrieking. "These are students! Poets! Teachers! Doctors! How can they make you stop bombing?"

General Ho stared. He didn't need better English to understand Gurney completely now.

Bill Borrows waved to the waiter, a big smile pointing to his glass, "Another! One for the generals too, please"

The Generals tripped over themselves to get out of Gurney's way as she bumped chairs towards the sticky black leather sofa in the main lobby. Julia followed, settled in beside Gurney.

Julia said. "Gurney, calm yourself. What we're seeing probably happens everyday here. The only thing different between today and yesterday is that now we know."

"Maung Ye must be dead," Gurney said.

"We don't know that."

"And Maung Naing must be in Thailand, in that hospital."

"You said he wasn't the type."

"Maung would have to do something."

A Burmese talk show, a man and two women having an animated conversation, filled the wide screen.

"You understand what they're saying?"

"I can't follow very well in a show like this." The young guest was explaining something about keeping insects out of the house, but Gurney didn't feel like explaining. She wanted her mother, she needed Maung Naing. She felt like a scared young girl and tried to push that feeling away.

"Time to get something to drink?" Julia asked. They tried not to drink while eating with the Generals.

"O.K.." Gurney dabbed her face with a tissue, blew her nose. A man in a long black jacket was on his way to serve them.

"Something strange and strong," Julia ordered, "We don't care what."

Robert and Bill were arguing across the hall.

Gurney stared at the large T.V. screen. She thought: I'm not brave enough or strong enough, even for simple things.

Julia eyed her thoughtfully, swirled the last of her drink. The waiter turned the volume of the program louder. It was the national news, Tatmadaw approved. "Come on now, don't be such a baby," Julia said, and looked Gurney over. "Are you sick?"

"I don't think so," Gurney said.

When Robert rejoined them his underarms were stained with sweat, his face flushed. "I'm so sorry Robert," Gurney said, blinking. Julia went to the bar for more napkins.

"Merger Gas isn't interested in my report," Robert went on. "I called corporate office. Turns out, I don't have authority even to sign papers! All along, this has been Bill's gig. He admits it. He just didn't want to do the legwork."

Gurney laughed at him, wiped her sleeve across her face.

She said, "God you are so innocent. Who couldn't guess that? No one gives up authority if they don't need to do."

"I quit my job," he told them.

"You what?" Gurney said.

"I've got to make my report," Robert said. "If Merger won't take it maybe I can deliver it elsewhere. Like, directly to the Merger shareholders."

Gurney wrapped her arms around his neck, pulled his scratchy face down to kiss it. "This whole trip," she said, "You've been my hero."

The sound in the room got louder and they all looked at the wide screen. Julia said, "National nightly propaganda, direct to you from Myanmar."

Gurney said. "Wow. Maybe Maung is going to get on the news tonight. That would blow his mind. It's almost impossible to get any kind of protest onto national news."

"Is this like a Myanmar edition of 60 Minutes?" Robert asked.

"Ha-ha, we wish," Gurney whispered. "We shouldn't necessarily believe everything we see. But look, there's the Grand Palace, and the Democracy Monument."

The camera was scanning monuments that Gurney recognized, and she gave them all a running commentary. "They're reporting the recent clashes on the border between rebel guerrillas and Myanmar and Thai military. They make it sound like there are no civilians on the border at all!" Dark images of Bangkok Hospital surrounded by Thai soldiers and military police filled the screen.

"What are they saying now?" Julia asked.

"I'm trying to figure it out," Gurney said. The sound was fuzzy. "Good thing it's happening in Thailand. If it was here, I'd be scared. 800 hostages! Imagine!"

The waiter adjusted the screen. Ashen-faced people were peering out hospital windows. The waiter bunched his forehead, tilted his head back. "And see there," he said and he winced, glanced over his shoulder to check who was listening. Bill Borrows was still drinking with the Generals.

"Look," he said again, "look there," and as he turned away, walked back to his station, on the big screen, a white cloth was waving out a hospital window.

"Okay," Robert said. "They surrendered."

"Robert," Gurney's eyes didn't move off the screen.

"I already got our flights," he said. "We leave 10 am tomorrow."

"But I don't get it," Julia said.

The camera zoomed past another glimpse of a white t-shirt on a stick, and then Thai soldiers rushing in front of the cameras towards a ragged group—Burmese men—coming out of the hospital, arms overhead. The camera scanned the thin exhausted faces, dark eyes.

"That's him," Gurney said. The camera had caught Maung's hopeful face, his shining, serious eyes. "Oh my God." Gurney clapped a hand over her mouth, laughing, crying. "That's him!"

But then, the shooting began. One after the other, the men fell backwards as though they'd rehearsed it. They were being executed by the Thai military on Myanmar's national nightly news. Gurney screamed. Bill and the Generals ran into the bar.

"Don't look!" Robert said, but it was too late. "You shouldn't look at this!"

Robert had Gurney in his arms. "That was Maung, Robert!" She sobbed. "They killed him!"

"They killed somebody," Robert said, "that's for sure," but he was as certain as she was of what they'd seen.

227

"It is a bloody goddamned world," Julia was saying. "Oh no. Don't look. Don't look." It was happening again in slow motion.

"Someone shut this fucking thing off!" Robert shouted.

Gurney's legs gave out from under her; Robert held her up.

General Than Te Ne said, "Thailand will keep the bodies for ten days, on display outside the hospital. So, you have time to go, and see your friends."

"Wow. That's just brutal," Bill Borrows said.

But the Generals shrugged their shoulders, and walked out of the room.

22.   Safety In Numbers

Somerville, Massachusetts January 25, 2000

Desmond drove into the financial district, and found a place to park. "Button up. It's bitter, bitter cold."

They zipped jackets, wrapped scarves around their faces, and approached the crowd. Half a dozen police officers were standing around.

"Overtime pay," Desmond whispered, and Bobby smiled.

Desmond spoke with an officer. "How's it going?"

"Cold," he said. "I'm calling it eight-hundred and three people, in honor of the triplets. Down by the corner of that building? Looks like triplets, to me."

Dreadlocks were swirling over drumming on buckets. People were dancing.

"That's one way to stay warm," Desmond said, but he covered his ears. It was loud. Tiny human bodies were dancing under tremendous puppet heads. They saw signs, like "democratize the Global Economy," and "No Race to the Bottom!" People were chanting.

"What are they saying?" Bobby asked.

"We want bread and roses too," Desmond said.

"I want bread and video games too," Bobby said this to be annoying, but Desmond didn't hear. The wind stung. Bobby saw Rickie, and was glad he was with Desmond.

"Over there," he told Desmond. "Down by the speakers. There's Rickie, and Mr. Hunt!"

They wormed their way through the frozen crowd.

"You didn't meet me after school today," Bobby said, and Rickie rolled his eyes.

"You're so weird," Rickie said. "You weren't where you said you'd be. I waited 'til five-thirty."

A big blocky guy came up to Desmond, stuck out a hand. Bobby recognized him. It was Hugh Moran's Dad. That meant Hugh was around here someplace. Mr. Moran asked Desmond, "Oh. You're a teacher?"

"No, I just coach basketball."

"Well I know you're not Bobby's dad," Mr. Moran said.

Bobby's parents had both met with Mr. Moran before.

"Yuh, well. I've got him for now. And you?"

"My boy Hugh is visiting his mother tonight. I thought you might be the real Dad. You look kinda like the kid here." Desmond seemed to have frozen in place. Mr. Moran added, "We live around the corner. I heard the drums."

"Hugh is visiting his Mom tonight?" Rickie said.

"Yeah," Mr. Moran said, "That's right, at the prison. In the mental ward at the prison, since you're so nosy."

"Mr. Moran, this is the art teacher, Mr. Hunt," Bobbie said, as though he was the one responsible for the confusion. "And this is my mother's cousin, Desmond. Mr. Hunt and Desmond are going to start coaching basketball together pretty soon."

Mr. Hunt acknowledged Desmond with a smile.

"So where are your parents?" he asked Bobby.

"I guess we can share the news now," Desmond said, "Since they'll be back home in a few days."

"Right," Bobby said. "They're doing research in Burma."

"Wow. Burma. That's very cool." Mr. Hunt's nose was bright red. The temperature was 9 degrees below zero. "Hot, I mean," he said. "It must be hot in Burma right now."

The drumming petered out and a speaker was introduced. He shouted into a microphone. "The WTO is a global shadow government of, for, and by corporations! Any globalization that occurs," the speaker said, and stomped, clapped his hands together, "should be of, for and by the people!"

"Your Mom would be thrilled to know you came here," Mr. Hunt said.

"I'm freezing," Bobby said. "I'm only here because Desmond made me."

"Right over there, inside that doorway," Desmond said, and gestured towards a little stone archway in a church, and a lighted area inside the door. Rickie's eyes were red and watery in the whipping wind.

"Bobby, can I come with you? I'm freezing too," Rickie said, and they ran together across the square. Bunches of people were huddled together outside, trying to get out of the wind. Inside, a heater was blasting in a hallway. They undid their coats.

"Awesome," Bobby said. The warmth felt like heaven.

"Awesome," Rickie repeated.

"Did Hugh talk about me today?" Bobby asked.

Now that he had Rickie alone, he dared to let him know: He was angry. He didn't trust Rickie or Hugh, he didn't like the way they made him feel. Feeling the cherry bomb now in his pocket, he was being the butt of their jokes. If Rickie and Hugh want to be friends, that's fine. But if they want to gang up on him, he'll give them a dose of reality.

"Are you kidding Bobby? D'you think he doesn't have a life? He could give a shit about you."

Bobby chewed on this for a minute. He said, "I didn't think wimps like you came outside, in cold like this."

"Nice Bobby. Right." Rickie said. He scowled and rubbed his hands over the hot air vent, stared out the etched glass of the door. "Like you're outside."

With Desmond nearby and the cherry bomb in his pocket, Bobby could afford to argue with Rickie. "I wouldn't say that Hugh doesn't give a shit about me. Maybe he thinks I'm the shit."

"Maybe," Rickie said. "But if Hugh Moran thinks you're the shit that's only because you think you're tough shit, calling him a huge moron and stuff in front of the whole class, and don't give me that shit anymore, you knew what it meant." And Rickie put both hands in his jacket pockets, the same way that Bobby had both hands in his coat pockets. "You know that word. You know huge anyway."

Bobby wondered if Rickie anything interesting in his own pockets tonight. After all, Rickie was the one who gave him the cherry bomb.

"Like I know you're a Dick," Bobby said, and though he'd thought of saying that many times before, he never dared till right then. But Rickie just stood, stomping around, waiting for his toes to warm up.

"I'm gonna smoke a cigarette," Rickie said. "I don't give a shit." And he pulled out a pack of matches and a butt, started puffing, clouding up the hallway.

"No smoking sign," Bobby pointed out.

"Shut up and leave me alone."

So that was it, Bobby thought. This dip-shit is a better friend with Hugh now. "Hugh really didn't say anything about me today" Bobby asked again.

"I already told you. No. Can you worry about something besides yourself" Rickie was smoking up the hallway. "Man I wish I never started smoking," he said. "Do you know how much these things cost?"

"I'm gonna go," Bobby said. But he might as well know the deal. "You gonna meet me tomorrow?"

Rickie coughed. "I guess so. But I also promised Hugh."

"Hugh? You asked Hugh to walk with us?"

"No, not with us, with me. But I said you might be there."

"Oh. That's interesting," and Bobby started walking around Rickie, one hand in each pocket, feeling the cherry bomb and the pack of matches in there. Rickie looked small, grayish white in the light.

"You don't have to walk with us," Rickie said. "I said it's up to you. I thought it was an opportunity..."

"Opportunity! I bet!" Bobby said, and he whipped out the cherry bomb and the pack of matches and held them up in Rickie's face. "I KNOW WHAT YOU'RE THINKING!"

It was immediately insane and ridiculous, but he leaned into it, like an actor in a play, like in a rap video, and he screamed and waved his hands rhythmically in Rickie's face, "I DON'T WANT TO WALK WITH YOU! STAY OUT OF MY LIFE!" and he ran back to Desmond, who was (fortunately) ready to go.

23. Freedom

Yangon Burma January 25, 2000

The sidewalk and roads were crowded, the air full of carbon dioxide and soot, and they both felt sick. Vendors selling umbrellas, brooms, radios, tablecloths, knick-knacks, spilled onto the street. His face came near hers and she turned, kissed him on the mouth. Of course, he thought, it's because now Maung is gone. Now, she doesn't have anyone else she loves.

Robert watched her shop. Gurney found a carved wooden elephant, the golden wood the very same color as her skin. The vendor, a tiny wrinkled lady in a wrinkled dress, a curly white dog in her lap , smiled an enormous smile black with betel root.

Robert got out his wallet. Gurney took the elephant for Desmond, and a hand-drum for Bobby. They admired the black and gray kittens prowling over the wares.

A sourpuss lady leaned over a table of shirts and lottery tickets, scowling, and Gurney bought two tee shirts from her. "One for you," Gurney told him, giving him back the change for his wallet. "And one for Bobby."

"Don't you think we should still stop in Thailand on the way home?" he was trying to talk her into it. "Pay our respects, visit the bodies. It's important to have closure."

"I don't want that kind of closure," Gurney said. "The body is not the man. The action is the man."

Maung's body, and the bodies of nine others, was in fact on display on the hospital steps in Bangkok. Gurney had placed several calls, spoken to an upset hospital administrator. No one was allowed to retrieve Maung's body. All they would be allowed to do is to view it.

The International Committee of the Red Cross was now involved and left them several messages at the hotel, inquiring about Maung Ye. Robert felt he and Gurney had pushed as hard as they dared for now. They'd be leaving Myanmar the next day, and until then, Robert was just trying to keep them from getting arrested and keep Gurney from completely falling apart.

Yet, Gurney's behavior was strangely more calm and even more loving than usual. He almost wished she would be angry again.

Outside the White Bridge International Business center, a crowd of foreigners had congregated.

"What's this? Some sort of convention?" Robert asked. "I wonder what they're doing? I thought foreigners were supposed to be getting out of the country?"

Several western businessmen mingled with Singaporean and Chinese-looking businessmen in crisp lightweight suits outside the main entranceway.

"Excuse me," Robert approached a white guy. "You speak English?"

"Sure." The man had a French accent, and was neatly dressed in a pastel pinstripe suit, beige shoes, and a brilliant white shirt. His face was tanned, his hair recently clipped. "How can I help you?"

"I'm just wondering what's going on. Is this a convention?"

"It's a seminar for organizations interested in doing business with Myanmar." The man had a bag of souvenirs under his arm. "The government is sponsoring it."

"Government?" Robert fumed inwardly. "But this is a military dictatorship. They've been bombing on the border. You've heard the warnings?" Gurney was squeezing his hand, but he ignored her.

"Oh. Don't listen to those reports, really," the man said. "If you never go to the bad areas, it doesn't really apply. In any case, it's an interesting seminar."

"What's your line of work?" Robert asked, and tried to be friendly. Maybe this was an opportunity to share some hard-won education with this idiot.

"I'm research representative for Premier Oil. We're part of a consortium building a pipeline through Myanmar."

Robert snorted. "That's funny, because I've been here doing research for Merger Gas, checking the working conditions on the pipeline."

"Well I hope they're good enough," the man said. "Premier is already good to go."

"They already did their research?" Gurney asked.

"Of the working conditions? Sure, of course. I'm not on that end of it. I'm more involved with sales. But there's momentum now, Thailand's agreed to buy at least 29% of the end product. No stopping it now."

"Why am I surprised to hear that?" Robert asked.

"It takes forever to get started, and then everything happens all at once," the man said. "'That's how it always goes."

Gurney tugged Robert's arm. "Come on," she said, and dragged him away. "We're wasting our time. Let's go back to the hotel. I need to lie down. I don't feel very well."

"I'm not an international business consultant anymore," Robert said. "I'm nothing."

"You're my husband," she told him. "And you're Bobby's father."

Robert answered, "Well, that's true." They kissed.

"We're a team," she said. "No matter what."

He said, "I know we are."

Back at the hotel, they tried calling Bobby. Across the hall, they could hear the Borrows' television going. In Boston, the phone rang and rang. Gurney and Robert both left "I love you" messages. Now they were together in the bed.

"I'm so sorry," he told her, and stroked the hair off her face.

"Stop being sorry," she said.

"But it hurts," he told her. "I know it's got to hurt."

"It's not that bad. Life hurts. You can't stop it from hurting."

"Life doesn't always hurt," he told her. "I wish right now you could just think about good things."

"I am. I'm thinking about the way good things all add together."

"Really?"

"Really," she told him. "I'm okay. I just don't have words for what I am thinking."

He massaged her temples, and said, "We can help each other through this. We can be brave."

"I know."

Faintly, they heard the news report being broadcast again.

Then the Borrows' television was abruptly shut off, and the silence that followed felt like it was in Gurney's body, too, dead on the steps. Robert said wrapped his arms around her, one hand on her belly, one on her breasts.

"I've been thinking," he said. "Maung could have killed hostages. He could have held up his gun, shot at the soldiers. But he surrendered. And that was the best thing anyone could do."

Gurney rolled towards him, the warmth of her body lifting the blanket like a gust of air. She worried aloud. "I must have driven you crazy. I've lived like a scared mouse."

"Well, how in the world could I ever work for a jerk like Bill Borrows?"

They pressed together, head to toe.

Robert said, "You've been pushing me to be a more honest person, to face my own truths. I appreciate that."

And then Gurney was on her back, Robert on his side, both staring at her hands as they made figures in the air.

"Robert," she turned to him. "I hope you can forgive me."

"For what?" he said. Though, he thought he knew. She'd tell him now how she'd always loved Maung. Gurney took a breath.

"Never mind, I don't need to know for what."

"For everything," she began. "For making your life more difficult than it would have been without me."

He took her hands, pushed them softly into the pillow over her head. "As soon as I saw you, I knew I wanted your kind of trouble."

Gurney rolled over on top of him, laughed at him.

"But maybe you shouldn't have married me so soon," she said.

"Maybe," he said, and regretted it the second it came out of his mouth. "Not when you were still in love with Maung." An ice machine made a racket in the hallway, but then their room was quiet.

"But I wasn't ever in love with Maung," she said, and a tear rolled down her smiling face, splashed onto his lip. "Not like I've been in love with you."

He could hardly bear to look at Gurney this way now, her beautiful face so close to his own, while she was looking at him through these particular tears. This was all he ever wanted, more than he ever expected.

"But I haven't been the best husband, have I?" Now that he'd found this little corner of truth, he explored it brutally, "In terms of being an inspiration, let's say, for you?"

"Oh, Robert, of course you have," she moved closer, whispered into his neck. "Incredibly inspiring. I am so inspired by you."

He said, "No, not really. I can see, I've just been making the motions," Gurney wrapped her arms around his head, hugged him closer, "even as your lover. I always wanted to be a better lover for you."

"Sex doesn't matter," she laughed.

"It mattered for you and Maung, didn't it?"

"Not really Robert. Did I say he was a good lover?"

"I thought you did."

"I exaggerated." They chuckled, weeping together.

Someone slammed a door in the hallway.

"Robert," she told him. "I believe in you." They breathed into each other, several long moments; wrapped fingers in each other's hair. He slid deeper into the bed, faced her, and pulled her body against him. It felt good to touch bodies like this. Good to notice how alive, how strong they each were.

She cried into his shoulder. "I've totally dragged you into the line of fire..."

"Hey Miss Drama Queen," he said, and kissed her belly. "Everybody's in the line of fire. Can you pass me another tissue?" He blew his nose.

They heard Bill and Julia exchanging sharp words, and the door across the hall slammed.

"Bill is such an asshole," Robert said as it occurred to him. "Does he still hit on you? I can say something to him now that he's not my boss."

She thought for a moment, and laughed, kissing his ear. "No, no," she whispered. "I'm okay. I forgive him."

Their window was open. Outside dogs were barking, roosters crowing. It was a full moon. The light made their faces deep and white, like ghosts.

"What are you thinking?" she asked him.

"That you're so strong," he said. "Amazingly strong."

She answered, "You're twice as strong as me."

And they stroked each other closer, took various portions of each other into their mouths, moved their bodies closer. In spite of everything, in spite of everything they knew and didn't know, in spite of a world full of obstacles, they loved each other.

In the morning when he woke up, she wasn't in bed. He opened his eyes. Light was coming through the curtains. Morning traffic had started up. Out of bed, but she wasn't in the shower.

Robert got dressed, went down to the breakfast buffet. Bill and Julia were having coffee and fruit salad. An alarm fluttered awake in Robert's stomach. He said, "Have you seen Gurney?"

"What?" Bill asked. "Is she gone?"

24.   Surrender

Boston January 26, 2000

In the morning, Bobby didn't want to go to school, and Desmond accepted this without discussion. Bobby listened as he made phone call after phone call after phone call. This was a complete one-eighty from the previous plan, and Desmond was letting every newspaper and magazine and radio station in the world know about what was happening.

Desmond had a disk with images of Gurney looking strangely beautiful, chained to the gates of the International Business Center. The disc had been delivered to the Red Cross by a group of Burmese schoolgirls. Gurney's public protest and subsequent disappearance was making international headlines.

"Don't come home till you find her," Bobby told his father when he called.

"Don't worry Bobby, I'm not leaving without your mother." He apologized, "At least I'm going to try not to."

But as the morning progressed, Bobby said, "Maybe I should go to school. I need to do something, or else I'm gonna start thinking she's dead or something."

"If you're up for it, you might as well," Desmond said. "That's what your mother would want."

And so Bobby left all his books, his lunch, everything but his cherry bomb and matches, and poked his head out the front door. No one was coming from either direction, and he was glad, because right then he didn't care to see any people. He didn't even like people. People can be so evil, so stupid.

He ran down the road, slipping on the soft wet snow that had fallen overnight, hands in his pockets. It was barely freezing today, January thaw.

As he jogged, he thought about his mother, because she was the family jogger. If she hadn't gone to Burma, she'd be jogging now. In a way, he was living the life she was supposed to be living. And he rounded a corner without slowing down because the light was in his favor, but one foot slipped into a slush puddle and the other on glare black ice. He went down with a splash.

Hugh and Rickie were coming across the road just in time to catch him down on the ground with his pants sopping wet. Rickie got him by one elbow and Hugh by the other before he had a chance to get out his cherry bomb. Ice water ran down his leg.

"Aw!" Hugh said. "That puddle got me, too. See?" And he showed Bobby his wet sneakers first, and then showed off his wet butt.

"Hey, we heard about your mom," Rickie said. "Her picture is in the paper. Wow."

"Yeah," Hugh nodded. "Yeah. I'd be scared. She must be pretty brave. Standing up to a dictatorship."

"Wanna walk with us?" Rickie asked. "Hugh's not a complete moron, are you Hugh?"

"Just a Moran. That's like, a few letter grades better than a moron." Hugh held out his hand. He looked worried. "We can shake hands and get over it, right?"

School was buzzing with news of his mother's disappearance, and every news report added new spins to the story. Some witnesses said she chained herself in the middle of a Burmese business convention, and chanted "Free Burma" until the police force came and took her away. The police denied the story, and said she must have unchained herself. But all anyone knew for sure was that now she was missing.

Newspapers and magazines kept calling the school, trying to get a hold of him for an interview. Mr. Hunt pulled him aside.

Mr. Hunt asked, "How're you holding up?"

"Okay," Bobby said.

"Is this a complete surprise Bobby? Did she warn you she was going to do something?"

Bobby had to think about that. "I'm not sure," he said. "She left a message on the phone the night before. She said she loved me, and told me not to worry. But that's what she always says." Since her disappearance, he'd listened to it over and over again. He'd practically memorized it, word for word. The anxiety that he'd been feeling all month long made sense to him now. "But yeah, I think she let me know," Bobby said. "I always knew."

"Knew what?"

"That she belongs to Burma."

Mr. Hunt said, "No, Bobby. She belongs to the whole world. We'll free her somehow."

A man with a camera was coming down the hall towards Bobby. "You don't mind?" The Principal trotted over and escorted the guy to the door.

Mr. Hunt said. "Call Desmond. If he's home, maybe he should come pick you up, get you out of here."

On the phone, Desmond told Bobby the media was there, too. "Since they've been booted off school property, now they're just waiting for you to get home."

"Would you just as soon face the gauntlet?" Mr. Hunt asked, "Or do you want to go to my house?"

"Nah, I'd better go back and help Desmond."

"I'll drive you then," Mr. Hunt said. "No book bag?"

"Nah," Bobby said. "Not today."

Out the back door, around the parking lot, a guy with a camera on his shoulder followed them until the principal came out.

And a live telecast van, dozens of reporters, cars, and two cruisers were blocking his street. All Bobby could think was, these people are assholes. They don't care about my mother, they don't care about me. They're only trying to make money, and I don't know what to say. He toyed with the cherry bomb in his pocket, and the packet of matches in the other hand, laughed to himself. Lighting and tossing it would be the easiest way to clear a path to his front door. He laughed a little more, remembering what his mother did, the time she set off one of the cherry bombs, and scared him and Rickie half to death.

"Do you think my Mom is alive?" Bobby turned to Mr. Hunt, when he stopped the car. "You don't think she's already dead, do you?"

Mr. Hunt pounded the wheel, looked over at Bobby. "I'm probably the wrong person to ask," he said. "I think we're all going to live forever."

Bobby got out of the car, reporters swarmed over. He closed his eyes. People can be so crazy. You can't really fight it. Bobby opened his eyes again and tried once more to look around, but it was too much. It scared him. All these reporters.

"I give up," Bobby said.

"Bobby, are you okay?" Mr. Hunt was out of the car, but Bobby was laying down on the sidewalk, surrendered to dozens of pairs of unfamiliar feet that stepped curiously around him, eyes squeezed closed against the flashing cameras. Then, Desmond was there, and he and Mr. Hunt were both carrying him up the steps.

25. Myanmar
July 2002

They brought her something to eat, sometimes dried fish in the rice, but not lately. At this moment in time, Gurney is watching a face: a square, hungry face. It's easier to look at a face, than to listen to its broken thoughts. And in the face, she sees a thousand faces. So many old people, brilliant people, gentle, thin field workers, those people who are afraid and rigid, who brutalize themselves and their neighbors, the mothers and fathers, the nurses and doctors and social workers and teachers, the government volunteers, the prisoners, warriors, farmers, and she starts to get a picture in her head, of the whole stunned world, and how no one really knows what they are doing, or why.

"You could have had anything you wanted," the face made her cry to look at it, and the body opened its arms, "You could have had democracy," as though this was a face that could even imagine democracy. Then re-shaping itself, she watched a guard crooking his arms, repeating another word several times before she understood he was speaking in English. "Freedom. You could have had freedom."

Professor Hyim's old apartment building housing the University transmitter, the shredded papers, the broken machinery that waited for her that day her father died: Gurney struggled to digest lost opportunities. But what is lost? Nothing if we are over and over again delivered from one life into the next.

"I believe in you," he'd told her. "I've always believed in you."

All that night with Robert, she'd barely slept. In the morning, the crowing roosters and barking dogs started before Robert opened his eyes. Gurney was awake for hours, sitting at the little table by the window, fully dressed, still deciding. They were scheduled to be on their flight at ten. It was barely dawn, bicycles just getting a head start on traffic, when Gurney took a horse cart out to the White Bridge, Ther Phyu.

The White Bridge isn't really a bridge at all. It's a causeway into the center of the lake, and it stops at The International Business Center.

Inya Lake stretched out serenely before her as it does for all of us, as though it has a consciousness of its own. An Intha man in a long boat rowed past, standing, the oar hooked around one leg. Pinks and silvers of dawn were streaking the air. An armed guard stood sleepily inside the door of the Center, watching her with his peripheral vision. It was an astoundingly beautiful morning.

A mobile band, that indomitable Burmese tradition, passed by in a carriage. Some of the musicians plucked a few sleepy notes, music jingling as they went down the road. Gurney dug into the bag that she'd been lugging around all morning, got out a bicycle chain and padlock.

The tourist/businessmen on the bridge waiting for the center to open its doors stepped aside as Gurney walked up, chain clinking in her arms. She acted as though she owned

253

the place, and they watched her loop it between the door handles of the business center, circle it twice around her waist, and clamp down the padlocks, before comprehending.

Maung used to say there were two sorts: Cutthroats, and people who could not be bought. Gurney was not a cutthroat. But five guys in uniform reached Gurney, examined her chain with hands on hips, complaining, shouting at her. The guard from inside the building finally found the rear door, hustled out, pointing his gun. He tripped, but didn't fall.

A group of Burmese children, baskets of flowers on their heads, ridges over their dark eyes, thanaka paste on their round cheeks, also saw her from the main road.

Gurney yelled at the top of her lungs, in English and in Burmese, for their sake, "Stop the massacres! Free Aung San Suu Kyi! Free the people!" She wasn't afraid even as the police broke the chain and beat her with it, even as they dragged her off the bridge, and threw her into the back of their truck.

Seattle, February 25, 2000 Massachusetts has lost its case in Federal Circuit Court and in a Federal Appeals Court. The decisions [against the Massachusetts Burma Law] have barred states from involvement in what the courts broadly defined as "foreign affairs." Such a broad ruling by the Supreme Court would also imperil laws that conflict with foreign trade relations under the 18 agreements of the World Trade Organization.

26.   Home

October 2002

When Robert and Bobby got back from the annual retreat at the Green Forest Monastery, it was still relatively early, and Bobby had plans to meet friends and play basketball. Robert was walking by himself outside the Italian market when he ran into Julia Borrows, who looked different, thinner, a bit older.

Julia said, "Just as I completely give up on it, here you are."

Robert opened his arms. "It's good to see you!"

Julia returned the hug, then stood away as Robert pulled the brown robe of the Buddhist sangha so it wrapped more closely around his body. They hadn't seen each other for nearly two years.

"You look good," Robert said. "Happy, healthy."

"I have to admit, I'm a little bit surprised," she hesitated, "to see you wearing that..."

"The robe? Not a big deal," he answered her. "The Buddhist stuff, it helps me." He laughed and shook his head. "It's not like I'm a priest or anything. I'm just a lay practitioner."

"Don't explain," she said. "It makes complete sense. I always thought the spiritual life would suit you."

"You did?" he answered, genuinely surprised.

"Well, you were into it before," she told him. The street smelled like pizza.

"I was?"

"I thought so." A cat ran across the road and into the alley. "You weren't?" As they walked along, even Boston seemed different, smaller, older.

Robert told her, "Well, the meditation was originally Gurney's thing. But since she's been gone, I've invested more in the practice. It's kind of ...the way I stay in contact. "

"You used to seem more nervous.."

"It's not exactly that there's nothing left to be afraid of," he said. "But I know now that being afraid doesn't make you safe. It's sort of a waste of energy, and I can't afford to waste any energy."

Julia linked arms with Robert, leaned her head on his shoulder as they walked, but she didn't reply. After a little bit, he said, "I think I found the place where they buried her mother. Most of the bodies claimed by the military in Rangoon were buried there."

"How'd you find out she's there?"

"I don't know. I just felt this presence." Robert let go of Julia, so she could catch a falling leaf. She grabbed it just before it landed.

"It doesn't sound weird," Julia said, "Sometimes I think I feel Gurney's presence."

"Like you're in contact with her?" he said. "Or like she died?"

She shrugged. They passed a group of old ladies waiting at a bus stop.

"How many times did you go back?" he asked.

"Once," she said. "Just that once."

A month after the disappearance Julia went back, accompanied by her husband, three lawyers from their company, and Senator Frank. The whole experience left a frightening taste in Julia's mouth, and she'd never wanted to go back again. "How many times did you go back?"

"Eight. I'm headed over there again next week, in fact. Even if we can't find anything new on Gurney, the other people in those prisons really appreciate the visit. Bobby and I've hooked up with Doctors Without Borders; we bring in medicine, bandages, stuff like that."

Julia rubbed her arms. "Gurney married a good guy," she said.

"I don't know about that," he said, "But I'm trying. After this trip, we're going to take a little break. Concentrate on Bobby's schoolwork for a while. If they said they had Gurney in jail, or even if the police would admit they once held her, but except for a few anonymous interviews, we haven't found a single lead. Not a person will step forward."

"The military is still hanging onto that same story?"

"Yup. They claim they never saw a thing. They say maybe she was abducted, maybe civilians hauled her off. They've investigated it as a crime, but found no suspects."

"You'd think another witness would speak up," she said.

"If it wasn't for the pictures," he shook his head. "We'd have no idea. That's our one miracle: that someone had a camera, and access to the Red Cross."

The sidewalk crossed under an overpass; the scent of pizza and lasagna and cooked garlic grew stronger and drifted with exhaust and soot from the highway. They walked along the row of shops (more pizza), crossed another busy street, and came to a small park, an old churchyard, with an alley garden. A flock of pigeons were pecking maple seed from between the slate paving stones. Boys wrestled with a basketball in a chain-linked court across the lawn.

"There's Bobby, and Desmond," Robert said. A pretty woman with shiny brown hair was there too.

"Who's that? A fan?" Julia asked. The woman screamed and applauded from the sidelines whenever Desmond came close to making a basket. Julia lifted her eyebrows.

"That's Desmond's new girlfriend," Robert said. "I think he's in love."

Desmond was bouncing up and down, pounding on his chest.

Julia laughed. "How nice! I'm sorry the Massachusetts/Burma legislation was derailed," she said. "But it looks like he's surviving the disappointment."

"His girlfriend is an activist too. And there's federal legislation she's working on. Desmond helps her with it. They have the right attitude. They don't discourage easily."

Bobby was dribbling the ball now, and he'd grown so much in the past two years, he was taller than Desmond.

"Such a combination of you and Gurney," Julia observed, and Robert nodded. Absorbed in the game, Bobby charged with the ball, yelling.

"He's a good kid," Robert said. "I'm proud of him."

Then they ran out of things to say, and watched all the jumping and screaming and throwing of the ball. From this distance the game had a likable intensity. They could see shots and near misses, hear the whoop of enthusiasm, but not sense the sweat or pain of exertion. From this distance, it looked effortless.

"I'm so sorry I couldn't do more," Julia said.

"I heard Bill had some problems. I know you did everything you could do.

Someone scored a basket. Desmond was doing his Tarzan-style chest thumping again.

"It was a nightmare," Julia admitted. "But we're sticking together," she added. "He seems to have new priorities, for now, at least."

"So I imagined," Robert told her. "I admire that. You probably saved his life."

"So did you," she added. "And Gurney." Leaves fell out of the trees and swirled in pretty colors around them and they bathed in the cacophony of the city, kids playing, traffic moving, a flag flapping on a flagpole.

She said, "I kept thinking we'd have something, some kind of closure at least. Not-knowing must be killing you."

"Nah," Robert said, but his face was somber. A quarter glinted against the ground and Robert bent over to pick it up. "What do we really know anyway?"

There were wrinkles around Robert's eyes that she'd never noticed before. His temple was slightly grayer, his baldness nearly complete. Julia touched his hand. "If there's anything I can do?"

Robert leaned back into the bench. "FYI, the insurance company sent me a death benefit for Gurney, based on the CIA report," he said. He spoke formally, his old professionalism shining through. "Gurney's been declared dead. But, Julia," he looked her in the eyes. "I'm not joking when I say she's not dead. And I'm not going to stop until I find her."

A car roared up onto the highway with a broken muffler, pushing a gush of warm air. The maple tree above them shook out a fresh rain of seeds.

"So what do you want me to do?" Julia asked him again.

"Just, believe that with me? Always. Believe she's alive, and that we're going to find her."

The roar of road noise passed, and now a plane was overhead. Julia patted Robert's sleeves, and he hugged her into his chest.

"Hey, no buttons to get tangled up in," he remarked.

She smiled. "We behaved ourselves pretty darn well over the years."

"I could always trust you to brush me off," he joked, and smoothed his robe. Leaves were still fluttering down. The sun was low enough in the sky to be blinding.

"But what are we going to do with all those burning desires now?" Julia asked, only partly kidding.

"We'll learn from them," Robert kissed her forehead.

"We cannot go on living in a fantasy world." ~ Aung San
Suu Kyi

27.   Border

Mya cooked rice in the can, and she gave the can to
Naw. Naw ate with her eyes closed. A dragonfly, swaying its
helmeted head, rested iridescent wings on Naw's smooth
forearm. Mya laughed. It took several moments, but finally
the dragonfly shuddered and un-clung itself, zooming away.

It was raining again, and they were huddled under the
banana leaves, burning a small fire to drive off mosquitoes.
An airplane was flying overhead. Watching the little girl eat,
hearing the plane fly overhead, it reminded Mya of
something. It reminded her of a kind of love, or a sort of grief,
that we all have. It is the sort of feeling she could hardly pull
apart. She was sensing something that binds us all together.
We might think of as a motherly feeling, or a wifely feeling.
But it's more than that .

No past, no future, no coming, no going. No here, no
there. A bird was singing. "Gurney, gurney, gurrrrneeeeee."

28. Aung San Suu Kyi

November 10, 2010

Pro-democracy heroine Aung San Suu Kyi, was released today after more than seven consecutive years of imprisonment in her decaying lakeside home. Guards removed the barbed wire that sealed her home from the street, and thousands of loyal followers burst through the streets to greet her, chanting, erupting in cheers, tears, and laughter.

It was an awesome and terrifying day for pro-democracy activists, who had feared for Aung San Suu Kyi's health amid reports that she was failing to eat or drink. Appearing thin and pale, she was smiling deeply and said, "I haven't seen you for a long time." A supporter held up a bouquet of flowers, and she took one, and wove it into her hair, and she climbed up on a stool, and insisted that the time for a democratic Burma had arrived. "United we can do anything," she said.

Aung San Suu Ky's release came just days after an election that was condemned by Western nations as a sham designed to perpetuate authoritarian control. It came 11 years after the death of her husband to prostate cancer, and nearly 11 years since she last saw her children. They are now young middle-age.

Born June 19, 1945, Aung San Suu Kyi was the daughter of Burmese political activists. Her father, Aung San, was a soldier/politician who founded the modern Burmese army and negotiated Burma's independence from the British Empire in 1947. Assassinated by political rivals when Suu Kyi was just a toddler, Suu Kyi also tragically lost her favorite brother, Aung San Lin, who drowned when she was still a young girl. Not many years later, her elder brother left Burma to become a United States citizen. When Suu Kyi's mother, Khin Kyi, was appointed Burmese ambassador to India and Nepal in 1960, Aung San Suu Kyi followed her there.

Suu Kyi went on to Oxford University and studied psychology, and politics. A devout Buddhist, she lived in New York City and worked at the United Nations for three years, fell in love with Dr. Michael Aris, (who was a scholar of Tibetan culture), and married him in 1972. Together they became the parents of two sons, blending English with Burmese Buddhist traditional education for their sons. In 1988 Suu Kyi returned to Burma to care for her ailing mother, and while there, she was enlisted to help lead the pro-democracy movement.

This was the summer of 8/8/88, when pro-democracy uprisings were brutally crushed by the military dictatorship.

265

The following winter Aung San Suu Kyi's mother died, and Suu Kyi vowed to stay in Burma and fight for democracy as her parents had done. Michael Aris and her children were still sometimes able to telephone her and sometimes able to see her, but by 1989 she was under the thumb of the dictatorship. Although barred from seeking office, in 1990 she won 82% of the national vote, and was placed under house arrest.

Aung San Suu Kyi was faced with the choice: live in exile with husband and sons in London, abandoning her nation and the pro-democracy movement, or sacrifice her family life in order to dedicate her life to a freer Burma.

She chose Burma, and won several human rights awards while under house arrest, including the Nobel Peace Prize. From Europe, her sons delivered acceptance speeches on her behalf, donating prize money according to her wish to establish a health and education trust for Burmese people. Since 1989, the Burmese junta refused to grant Alex or Kim Aris visas to visit their mother

Today, Aung San Suu Kyi acknowledged that the choices she made were hard on her sons. They were separated from her at just 11 and 15 years of age. When her husband was diagnosed with terminal prostate cancer in 1997 the Burmese government still refused to grant Aris a visa, saying that they did not have the facilities to care for him, and urged Aung San Suu Kyi to leave the country to visit him. She stayed in Burma, believing that she would never be allowed to return if she left.

Michael Aris died in March 1999 on his 53rd birthday, having seen his wife only five times since 1989. This is the speech she gave from National League for Democracy Headquarters in Burma, within 48 hours of her release from house arrest.

Speech upon her release November 12, 2010, by Aung San Suu Kyi

I'd like to start out with word of thanks. We haven't seen each other for so long. But, no matter how long it has been, I'm very pleased and encouraged to see we all still remain strong. In order for us to do what we want to do ... we do know what the people want. But it is more important to know how to get what we want. In my view, politics is learning. We must learn. I said repeatedly when I talked to young people that I don't believe in such thing as smart or dull people, good or bad people, I only believe in whether one is teachable or not teachable. I do believe our people are teachable. It's not enough for us to only desire for something. We need to know how we are going to get what we want, and how to get it in the right way. Why is it important to get it in the right way? I'm not saying as if I were perfect. If we don't do it in the right way, no matter how good our goal is, our journey will get twisted and eventually our goal will be destroyed. Therefore, we must get what we want in the right way. I know there are many questions that people want to ask us. We also would very much like to hear (Burmese) people's voices.

I've been observing and learning peoples' desire, what they want every single day. Wouldn't it boring to be listening to the radio for 5, 6 hours a day? But in the name of the people, I've been listening everyday. By listening like that, I think I know what the people want to some extent. I don't mean I know everything. And I can't know everything either. I welcome people to talk to us. Only then, we would know what we can do for our people. Without the participation of people, nothing can be achievable. Whatever we do can be achievable only with the peoples' participation. Only with such attitude (and determination), I believe we'll be able to reach our goals smoothly and in the right way. That means, we will have to do a lot of work. Without work, we won't get anything. We Burmese often say it's just because of "karma." So I have asked youth repeatedly if they know the meaning of "karma." "Karma" is basically doing. So when you say yourself it's because of "karma," then it would mean it happened because of what you did. So if there is something we want, we must try to make it happen.

We can't persuade people by telling them we will do something that is impossible. We will all build the road toward democracy together, we'll build together, and we'll walk together. This is the only way to reach the goal we want. We'll have to do it with a willing heart. We can't do it half-heartedly. We can't wait for other people to build it for us. As you all come and gather here, I know you come here and support with hope. The burden of hope is not small. It is a big responsibility to shoulder hope. But I'm not afraid of being responsible. There is only one thing I'm afraid of. I'm afraid that I don't fulfill my responsibility. I will try to fulfill my responsibility till the end. In trying, I would like the people to give us advice, assistance, and point out if there is any issue. Address any issue to us properly and genuinely. Doing so would help us achieve the goals we all want. May I make a request to the people? When you work with us, please do it openly and boldly. Don't worry whether you should say this or that. You can feel free to tell us whatever you like. If we disagree, we'll of course have to say so, because it is the fundamental of democracy.

Freedom of expression. Freedom of expression isn't the same as freedom of yelling. Of course, sometimes, it might involve some anger. But it's very important to build understanding among one another.

We must exchange our thoughts and views. For that, we'll have to train ourselves and practice it. Now I see everyone is using (mobile phones). It shows improvement in communication. Make good use of this to build understanding and unity among one another. Please raise your hands those who have mobile phones. Let's see how many. Wow …. many people are now using mobile phones. For me, I just got a chance to use such phone for the first time today. In the past, we didn't have those yet.

(In responding to the sign "We love Su"
  ………………)

What is the meaning of love? It's not enough just saying "love" per se. We have to do the work. Love is willing to do to keep each other happy.

Please feel free to send us letters. If you worry mails might get lost, just come and drop it here (at NLD headquarters where she was giving his speech). I'd like to know what you have in mind. Over the last 6,7 years, I want to know what has been in peoples' mind, what in their mind has changed? I can't know right way. I'll have to take time and learn. I'd like to talk to everyone but it's practically not possible. If I could, I would have talked to everyone but it'll never end. I do want to talk to people. Standing alone and only one talking is so boring. You talk and I respond vice versa would be more lively, productive and valuable. If there is only one person talking and the rest are just listening, I don't think it's in line with democracy.

We need to have peoples' "hit-taing" (meaning a place where people can vent emotions, desires, complaints, what they have in mind) Thank you for being patient and waiting here for so long. If I am speaking like this for long, I think people will also get tired.

You're tired for over 20 years so you're probably getting used to it. Tiresome is not a problem. But what's important is if it's worth getting tired at all. We must use our energy in a way so that it's worth getting tired.

Now I'd like to say to you this. Don't loose heart. Sometimes, you might get depressed looking at our country ....saying we haven't reached anywhere yet and there isn't still any progress yet. But don't get depressed. We must have perseverance. We must persevere in whatever we do, until we reach the goal. There is no such thing as work that is done. If one task is done, there will be another. So this applies to building a nation . We'll have to do one thing after another. In life, there cannot be a complete satisfaction. But we certainly need to reach a certain degree of satisfaction. For that, we must all work together. It's not possible if we don't work hard so. I can't say I will do (everything. But if there is participation, trust and support, our effort will be more energized. I will work with the peoples' efforts. I can't do alone. I don't want to do it alone either.

I have no intention at all to do it all alone. I

will work with others, I will work with our fellow men and women in the country, and with our fellow men and women around the world who support us with genuine hearts. We will all work together to reach the goal we want. We must anchor this firmly in our hearts and souls.

Courage, as some might think, is not something like going in the front, raising their fists in anger or in a show of defiance. Courage is something we make efforts tirelessly with a strong determination to make what we want happen in reality. We have to nurture such kind of courage.

Really courage is something we do on daily basis. Our people (of Burma) have to be courageous to face each day. We must make good use of our courage, for the people and for the country, not just for oneself or one's own family. I want to say this repeatedly. Also, don't hold the attitude that we have nothing to do with politics. I have said this since in the past … that … we can probably say we have nothing to with politics, but politics will come to do with you. We can't avoid it. Everything is politics. Alright? Not just who come here and support us. That woman staying home cooking is also politics, because they have to work with the budget they have. So it's also politics. Struggling for the well being of your children is also politics. Everything is politics. No one can avoid politics. Those who say they have nothing to do with politics and that they don't want to participate in politics are those who don't understand politics. So try to understand politics.

Please also guide us. We have to learn from one another. The people and the democracy activists must guide us so that we won't make mistakes. There is one thing important about democracy, and that is, those who follow should be able to, must have a right to keep accountable those who lead at the front. And that is democracy. The general public should be able to keep accountable those who govern (who are also minority in numbers). This is democracy. For us also, we are willing to be guided by the people.

Let me tell you this. During my time of being detained, I had to deal with security guards. They had been good to me. They did treat me properly. This is the truth that I'm telling. As we know we must thank those who we owe. I am thankful for the ordinary security staff who treated me well. I'm saying this with a sincere heart.

Many might wonder how and where our political journey will go. We will work toward national reconciliation. To me, I certainly don't have a certain people/group that I can't work with. Whoever it is, we can work if there will a willingness to work things out. We can talk if there will a willingness to talk. We will continue to go along this line. For that, we do need peoples' energy and support. Whatever we do or decide, we'll let the peoples know. For now, we, within NLD, haven't had a chance to sit down and have a proper discussion yet. But we will work with not only NLD. I'd like to work with all groups that are working toward democracy. And the people need to surround these efforts. We'll have to tell the people, explain to them. Sometimes, there might be issues where people will not agree with what we do. Not every single one can have the same opinion. The ability to work together despite disagreements is also a fundamental of democracy. Why do we have to do it? We will have do it, in order to gain trust and understanding from the people, not the same as trying to get votes from the peoples. (Audience laugh ....)

We will continue to work with the trust, understanding and support from the people. I do apologize that for the time being, I can't tell you exactly what we will continue to do. If I had told you that I would do anything immediately after I've been released, it would sound like I'm speaking without prudence and reason.

In the meantime, we'd like to hear from the people as much as possible. By listening to the people, we'll decide how we will continue to do our future work. But as I said before, we'll work with peoples' support, and we'll work together with all the groups that are striving for democracy in order to achieve national reconciliation in our country. We'll work toward national reconciliation to cause least possible pain to the people. I can't guarantee however that there will be no pain. Sometimes, we do have to bear pain. We do suffer and our colleagues do suffer. But we'll try our best to seek out ways that will least hurt the people. If there is any pain involved at all, I'd like to request you in advance to remain tolerant. Regardless, we must do the work. It is not possible that we only want something but we don't want pain.

We must be able to distinguish between what's right and what's wrong. We must have the courage to stand on the side of righteousness. What is right and what is wrong cannot be the same all the time. As time changes, as circumstances change, answers (solutions) also change. But, whether we should or should not do, we should ask our conscience.

There is one thing my dad used to say. He said he dares to stand in front of his own court of conscience for a trial. For me to, I do stand in front of my own court of conscience daily to be trialed. Likewise, our fellow peoples should also stand before your own court of conscious daily and get trialed. If you do so, the answer to which whether you are really doing what you ought to do will appear and become clear. If we all do so, our efforts will gain value. We must use our energy and strength in the right way. No one can destroy the power of using (our) strength in the right way. Please take a note of that.

Let's test the spirit of consideration, understanding and good heart of our peoples here. Let me try it a little bit, ok? People far over there are shouting because they can't hear well. I'm also about to finish my speech. So, those who are at the front... would you please move to the side and make a space so that those who are at the back can come over in here closer.

Aung San Suu Kyi

9406888R0

Made in the USA
Lexington, KY
24 April 2011